LIKE THE GREEKS DO

PETER SCHUTES

CONTENTS

LIKE THE GREEKS DO

PART I
HERCULES AND LIPPOS

PART II
THE GOSPEL OF PRIAPUS

PART III
ONE ETERNAL DAY

LIKE THE GREEKS DO

I

HERCULES AND LIPPOS

INTRODUCTION

In the ancient world, the ideal of male beauty included a smaller-than-average penis. Men with big penises were considered ugly, brutal, and undesirable. The modern world has allowed for a much broader definition of beauty. Now men may be admired for any number of reasons, whether it is for their delicate features, their brusque visage, their small penis, or their massive prick. I would venture to say, however, that the masculine ideal now tends towards muscles and a larger-than-average penis. Hercules was big; Lippos was massive. Rejected by women and men alike, they found acceptance in each other's embrace. Here is their story.

✿ I ✿

BIG LID, GIANT POT

There is a lid for every pot.

Mighty Hercules didn't believe he could ever find a pot big and durable enough for his powerful lid. The Greek hero had the strength to move mountains and divert seas but could not find a mate. Women were far too fragile for him. He needed to grab, squeeze, and pound. No woman could tolerate his powerful thrusts. Boys and men were too fragile to handle his intense grabbing and pounding. So Hercules remained celibate, turning all his frustration towards the heavy boulders and logs he lifted and carried to town, where he sold them. Boulders were a precious commodity in Greek culture. A boulder in one's garden was a status symbol, and they fetched a high price.

Hercules peddled stone and wood to make his daily bread. And each day, his muscles grew more powerful, and the nipples on his chest grew further apart as his pectoral muscles swelled. He had the kind of butt upon which one could rest an urn of water. Jutting out like a shelf from the small of his back, it was a marvel to behold from any angle.

Hercules had a normal family, or so he thought. He didn't know his father was Zeus. His mother, Alcmene, had been tricked. Zeus appeared to her disguised as her husband, Amphitryon, and gave her a child. She had later learned that Amphitryon had been out drinking all night, so he couldn't have been the father. It was an impostor, but that was all she knew. And she never breathed a word to anyone, least of all her bastard son.

As he matured, Hercules gained incredible strength. His cock gained in size and girth. He had a big dick, but it wasn't so big that a woman or man couldn't accommodate it. It was the thrusting power of his back muscles that caused women to run from him. He shoved so hard it felt like a hammer in their birth canal. Men, too, balked at Hercules and his flesh mallet. He got to third base but couldn't persuade anyone to go farther.

When the Athenian navy came to town looking for conscripts, Hercules signed up. He was trapped and frustrated, and the military seemed like a good way to get away from the village of his youth. His parents, fearful of the war with Sparta, pleaded with him to stay, but Hercules needed adventure. The training camp was near Piraeus, the Athenian port. After asking directions, Hercules found his way to the naval headquarters.

The first day of training was brutal. Hercules, a seasoned wrestler, had no trouble with hand-to-hand combat. He was a terrible archer, though. He was physically strong but not precise. He could send an arrow flying at very high velocity, but with no aim, it would sail into nothing. His brute strength and his well-made armor assured him a position as an epibatai, a soldier of the sea. But he would never be an archer.

In the humble barracks, the other cadets gave Hercules a wide berth. The sight of the hulking muscleman strutting through the room was unnerving. Everyone was disgusted to see that he had a massive penis under his tunic. Well, nearly everyone. In his time, a small penis was considered a sign of great intelligence and gentleness. Hercules displayed neither trait.

The size of Hercules' body was more than double

that of the next most muscular man, Thraxos, the boatswain. Thraxos had been blessed with a tiny penis. Women yearned for him, not a brute like Hercules. When Thraxos flexed his legs, his penis disappeared between his thighs. "I'll bet you wish you had a small one like mine."

Hercules laughed to himself. If they only knew how good it feels to have a substantial chunk of meat swinging between your meaty thighs.

In another row of bunks, the men were whinnying like horses. They were mocking him! Hercules turned, angry, only to see that they were not mocking him but Lippos, a slight young man taking a sponge bath. They nicknamed him "Hippos" or "Horse". The youth's face was bright red with anger. Hercules didn't know why, but he felt a need to protect the kid. Then he saw it. It was soft, running the length of the man's thigh, ending at a point midway between his knee and his ankle. It was as thick as Hercules's powerful wrist, perhaps even thicker—poor fellow.

"Hey guys, quit that. Can't you see he's upset?"

The mob turned angrily, but upon seeing the dark shadows painting Hercules's face, their anger changed to fear.

"Leave him the fuck alone!"

The crowd scattered. Hercules put an arm around the lad.

"You and me, we share the same problem." The muscleman gestured to his own penis, which was growing larger now that he had given it attention.

Lippos ducked out from under Hercules's bulging arm. "You have no idea what it's like to have a problem like mine!"

The shorter man ran out of the barracks into the underbrush. Hercules pursued him. He found him in a glade of trees. Hercules grabbed the kid by his waist and pulled him close in a bear hug. To his astonishment, he felt the short guy's cock growing hard against his thigh. Hercules had a trapped hard-on as well.

Lippos looked into Hercules's eyes. A bolt of lightning flashed in the distance. Hercules felt a deep friendship with the young man. It was more than friendship; it was mutual erotic love. Having never felt anything like it, Hercules encountered a mixture of emotions: guilt, lust, fear, excitement, and some he couldn't name.

Hercules lowered his head and planted a kiss on the boy's mouth. Lippos returned it. He began to cry.

"What is it?"

"I want to fuck you, but no one will have me."

Hercules chuckled at the thought of the younger man penetrating his virgin hole. "And I want to fuck you, Lippos, but my thrusts and hugs are too powerful. I will break your bones or your ass or both."

Lippos shook his head. "I know a way. Come on"

He led Hercules to a grassy knoll. The hulk scratched his head.

"What are you planning? I don't get fucked."

Lippos put a finger on Hercules's lips.

"Lie down, face up."

The muscle man reclined, his big meat pole wobbling in the breeze.

There were sprigs of unknown herbs growing in the grass. Lippos searched and found one with oily flowers. He squeezed the oil onto his palm, then rubbed it in his hole. He squeezed again and rubbed the oil on the muscle man's pole.

"I'm telling you, Lippos, I can't control my hips. I'll break you. But as he said this, Lippos had already placed the brutal cock inside him.

"Stay still. I'm driving." And drive, he did. He bounced up and down, using his knees for leverage. He rose to the point where Hercules was close to falling out of the hole, then forcefully sat until the cock hit the rear rectum wall. He repeated this several dozen times, and then he did a trick. He twisted to the left, allowing Hercules to enter his sigmoid colon.

"Oh. Are you hurt?" Hercules was worried he had torn the boy apart.

"Relax, Hercules. You're past the second hole. Now you can thrust as hard as you want."

Hercules bucked, sending Lippos skyward. The boy crashed back down on the massive cock, letting it snake through his rectum with ease.

Hercules held the boy as he stood, so he could fuck standing up like he had long dreamed of doing. With violent thrusts, he swiveled and thrust over and over.

"Yes!" Lippos howled with delight. "Don't stop. Right there, oh yeah, right there."

The words made Hercules tingle at the base of his balls. He churned out a double helping of pre-ejaculate, lubricating the boy's rectum. He was close. Almost as if in response, the shorter man oozed the same slick liquid on Hercules's calves and toes.

Hercules grunted repeatedly. "Oh shit, I'm gonna come."

Lippos licked and sucked those giant nipples, which sent Hercules home."

"Unnnnnnh! Ooooooh!" Hercules felt his sperm filling the boy to overflowing. The last few spurts wouldn't fit, and they sprayed back onto his belly as they shot past his cock and out the exit.

The two lay in the grass, kissing and playing with each other's bodies. After an eternity, they returned to the barracks.

INJURIES

The cadets were naked, sponging themselves to remove the sweat and mud of the day. Only a few had heavy cocks. Most cadets were blessed with the tiny penises that women treasured so much. Lippos was in a cot several rows over. As he left Hercules's circle of protection, the whispers began and grew into jeers. This time, they called him "Tripous" or "Tripod." The jeers grew in intensity until everyone on his aisle shouted a cruel rhyme: "Lippos o tripous phallos tou hippos!" or "Lippos the tripod, hung like a horse!"

A loud crack came from the top of the aisle. Hercules was banging heads together, rendering the men unconscious. He marched down the aisle, knocking heads like a game of stones.

The tormentors fled in terror, retreating to the latrine or the next building over. Hercules put his pack down on the bed next to Lippos.

Hercules unshouldered his bag, revealing a shield, a sword, and a complete set of armor. "I'm a marine, and I need an attendant." He lay on the bed, staring hungrily at the young man.

"I'm already conscripted to Kratos, the man whose bed you occupy now."

Hercules put his hands behind his head and stared up at the ceiling, feeling his member stiffen from the memory of what they had just done. "No matter; I'll set him straight when he comes around."

He drifted into a dreamless sleep, only to be shaken awake by the ugliest man he'd ever seen.

"Hey! Asshole! You're in my spot."

"Your spot is over there now." Hercules gestured to his original bed.

"There is no room for my attendant there."

"Find a new one, Kratos; this boy is mine."

Kratos had expected this. He pulled a dagger from under his cloak and attempted to plunge it into the muscle god's heart. As if striking an iron door, the dagger bent and bounced off Hercules.

"Looks like you'll need a new attendant and a new dagger. Now buzz off."

Hercules winked at Lippos, who stared at his new guardian with a mixture of love, admiration, and lust. He licked his lips unconsciously as Hercules got hard.

The military had no laws against cadets fucking. Rape was not tolerated, but anything two men could dream up together was fair. Judging by the noises all around, Hercules figured many of the new recruits were getting their first taste of oral or anal pleasure.

He looked across at Lippos, the diminutive beautiful young attendant, and wiggled his thick cock in the air.

Lippos started with a valiant attempt to get Hercules to fit in his mouth. Only the top third of the head fit. It grew much fatter at the corona. Lippos was too small to blow Hercules. So he did what had worked before. This time, an ampoule of olive oil provided the needed lubrication. Lippos straddled the bed, standing with his impossibly long, thick limp cock draped across Hercules's chest. With his hand, standing on tiptoe, he placed the top of Hercules's massive cock at the rear entrance. He drizzled olive oil along the length of the shaft and rubbed it in. He used a sheep's bladder to squeeze a nice amount of oil inside his rectum. Lippos sat slowly on the throbbing cock, letting it stretch him wide. The pounding sex from earlier had bruised him slightly; he winced as the head poked past the second hole. He rode up and down, letting the cock glide in and out of his colon. He was still quite loose from their earlier dalliance. Hercules couldn't believe his good fortune. Leaving his small town had been the best decision of his life.

Lippos's cock began to stir. It straightened and lifted gently, fighting gravity as best it could. A droplet of clear semen threatened to fall on Hercules's face. The muscle man stretched his neck and lapped up the boy's juice. Lippos doubled down, forcing the brute's cock as deep as it could go, then using his knees to lift off of it, never letting it escape his insides. Hercules sucked on the tip of the giant throbbing wand of flesh. Lippos surpassed Hercules in both length and thickness. Hercules had a big mouth and a great tolerance for pain. He inhaled the head and the first few inches of Lippos's member. The more he sucked, the better it tasted.

"Oh, Hercules, that feels so good!"

It occurred to Hercules that Lippos may never have felt the inside of a mouth on his cock. Only a robust and powerful man could take the monster in his mouth. The giant cock began to drool. The slick dribble was a lubricant, making it easier for Hercules to take more of it past his tonsils. The room around them was filled with pairs of men doing similar things, but none were as muscular as Hercules, and they weren't impossibly hung like Lippos. They had formed a circuit of cock and flesh. Hercules pounded his way into Lippos, and Lippos snaked his way down the throat of the muscle god.

Hercules felt the tingling in his balls that meant he was going to come in the next few minutes. Then, without warning, while lodged deep in Hercules's throat, Lippos ejaculated. Hercules could feel the hot come as it shot straight to his stomach. He wanted to taste it. He relaxed his neck. The head of the cock was still inside the gaping mouth of Hercules. Hercules tasted the salty-sweet come. It was a feast. It turned him on even more. When Lippos had spent his last drop, Hercules sucked out the dregs before letting the heavy head landed with a loud thump on his chest. With great force, perhaps a little too much, he thrust himself rapidly in and out of Lippos. Within seconds, he had an orgasm unlike any he had ever known. The big fat dick just kept spurting and spewing more and more come inside the boy until there was so much it could only spurt out along the edge of the anus. Hercules felt his own come puddle in his groin.

When they kissed, Lippos could taste sperm, his sperm, in Hercules's mouth.

When Lippos stood, his soft cock swinging gently below his knees, he staggered. Hercules caught him. Lippos was still draining come out of his ass, but it was now mixed with blood. The burly demigod hoisted Lippos onto his shoulder and rushed him to the medic. The medic melted waxed linen and put the dressing over the boy's stretched and torn hole.

Hercules paced outside the doctor's tent, muttering curses and smacking himself fiercely on the forehead. He had done so well with Lippos, but now he had hurt him. He would be lucky if the guy even looked at him again.

The doctor motioned Hercules in. He came to the bedside where Lippos was recovering. The young lad reached out a thin arm and stroked a giant bicep.

"Hercules, that was too—"

"Too much, I agree. I'm sorry."

Lippos frowned. "No, I was going to say that it was too good. We are going to have to try new things to surpass it."

"But I hurt you." Hercules was surprised the kid wasn't planning a breakup.

"It was a wonderful pain. I have never come in someone's throat before. Having your big cock inside me made it better." Lippos blushed as he explained.

Hercules said, "I didn't think it felt good. Doesn't it hurt to have me inside you?"

Lippos shook his head. Hercules raised a pensive eyebrow. He had always seen the passive man as a martyr to pain for another man's pleasure. It never occurred to him that it might feel good.

The Doctor told Lippos to stay still and that he would check him in the morning for any further bleeding. Hercules returned to his bed. It smelled wrong. In the faint light, he could see a horse turd on his pillow. He knew it had to be Kratos. Silently, he carried the pillow over to where Kratos was sleeping. He held the ugly man's head and pulled out the pillow from under him, replacing it with the horse shit pillow. He crept back to bed with his clean pillow and chuckled himself to sleep.

TURNABOUT

Hercules awoke to hear Kratos shouting in a rage. He locked eyes with Hercules.

"You! I'll make you regret that."

Hercules laughed. "I'd like to see you try." He stood up and flexed his back muscles to spread his chest nearly twice as wide. Kratos could say nothing in reply.

Hercules rushed to the doctor's tent to find him removing the linen dressing from Lippos's hole. The blood was gone.

Lippos now had a loose, stretchy rectum. Hercules stuck a finger in just to feel how soft and loose it was. Lippos wriggled with desire. "Not here, not now. Later."

Hercules reluctantly withdrew his thick finger from the bum of his hyperetes (assistant). "It's just so fleshy and loose, like a vagina."

Lippos gave a mischievous grin. "Wait until you see what I do to yours! It's going to look like you gave birth."

Hercules frowned. He didn't want a painful cock in his ass, let alone the monster Lippos was swinging. He stopped to think. He remembered how much he liked when Lippos pushed into his throat. It didn't hurt - but Hercules was nearly immune to pain. As he pictured the serpentine cock entering him from behind, he felt a rush of blood to his groin. He was getting hard thinking about getting fucked. And he wanted it.

"We'll see, Lippos. You may get your wish tonight."

The doctor, who was eavesdropping, said, "Lippos really shouldn't have intercourse up there for a few weeks. You may want to switch roles."

Lippos laughed all the way back to the barracks.

After the lanterns were extinguished, Lippos crawled into bed with the massive muscle god and a crock of butter. He greased up his index finger and started to work his way into the beast of a man.

Hercules involuntarily clamped shut, nearly breaking Lippos's finger.

"Relax. Push out, don't clamp down."

Hercules did as instructed, freeing the finger to penetrate further. Soon, it was buried to the knuckle. Lippos slid it in and out, causing Hercules to moan.

"Am I hurting you?"

Hercules laughed as he shook his head.

"How about now?" Lippos inserted a second digit and then a third.

"Keep doing what you're doing. It feels so good." As he said this, Hercules wriggled his tight, round bottom closer to the lad.

In another minute, Lippos worked his pinky and thumb inside. He punched past the inner sphincter until ass muscles engulfed his slender wrist. He took care to tap on the prostate, which caused Hercules to groan with pleasure.

"Deeper!"

Lippos obliged. He was elbow-deep inside Hercules's digestive tract. Then, with a seesaw motion, he pulled out and pushed in. Hercules writhed on the bed, dribbling clear sticky liquid from his half-hard penis.

"Unhh, I want you inside me. Fuck me!" Hercules pounded the straw mattress for emphasis."

Lippos pulled out his greasy arm. He applied liberal

amounts of butter to his giant cock. He had been inside a few brave young men, but none got him so hard and excited as Hercules. He was fucking a demigod, though no one save Zeus and Hera knew it.

"Hurry! I need you in me now!"

Lippos was astonished as the muscular ass swallowed his massive cock head. He pushed further. Hercules reached behind and pulled the boy closer until they were locked to the hilt. Never had Lippos entered a man so quickly and so completely.

"Now, do it!"

Hercules would always be the boss, no matter what position he was in. Lippos obeyed, rocking his hips back and forth, growing even bigger and harder, until he touched the descending colon.

That was the magic spot. Hercules gushed clear precome as he moaned to the gods in thanks for making such intense pleasure possible on Earth.

Lippos watched a bead of sweat crawl slowly across Hercules's back. He leaned forward and licked it. The sweat was infused with manly flavors that caused Lippos to grow stronger and more virile. He thrust with tremendous power, punching the descending colon with force.

Hercules rolled over onto his back so he could admire the face of the beautiful boy filling him so completely. He wrapped his powerful legs around Lippos's waist. The boy responded with redoubled strength. He watched as the eyes rolled back in Hercules's head. Loud moans echoed through the quiet barracks.

Lippos said, "Oh shit. I'm close."

Hercules nodded fiercely. "Me too."

Whatever that drop of sweat had done to Lippos, he was unprepared for just how powerful it was. The come gathering in his balls felt thicker and hotter than he had ever known. He licked more sweat from Hercules's inner thigh. It sent him over. Ejaculate flew out of him, painting the insides of Hercules. It was burning hot and had the consistency of honey.

Hercules opened his mouth in astonishment. His own semen flew out of his cock and landed in his mouth, in his hair, on his eyelids, his cheeks, and his chin. He was full of thick gooey boy come and covered in his own manly effluence. They kissed with the passion of a newlywed couple.

The barracks broke out in applause. Lippos blushed as his serpentine cock uncoiled out of Hercules. Hercules just rested on his back while his musclebound ass expelled a river of thick semen; he was too content to knock heads. The jeers died down. The two lovers slept in each other's arms.

AT SEA

The naval training was easy for Hercules. He tore through the strength exercises and outran every cadet. Lippos, who had struggled initially, was fast becoming a top cadet, even though he was not a marine. His nightly expeditions into the bowels of Hercules gave him a steady supply of the enchanted sweat he craved almost as much as the sex. Never in his life had he been strong like this. It was intoxicating.

But even more thrilling was the joy Lippos got when Hercules's big ass engulfed his dick, taking it easily to the root. He had never been with a man or woman who enjoyed his girth, which increased with his arousal and brought most people terrible pain. Hercules was immune to such pain. He would moan with delight as Lippos thickened inside him. It was a virtuous circle because Hercules's moans made Lippos even more excited, causing his cock to swell yet again.

Hercules, muscular and overflowing with testosterone, was the picture of manliness. But when Lippos ran a hand across the demigod's bottom, Hercules became a lovestruck girl. One squeeze of the gluteus maximus, and Hercules was ready to lay back and take it like a woman.

Lippos, initially thin and slight but quickly growing thick and strong, had believed he was doomed to be the woman because nobody could take his oversized cock. Now, tethered to the insatiable muscleman, he had never felt manlier. He was the top dog in his relationship with Hercules.

The blissful days of basic training were rudely interrupted when word came from Mytilene that The Spartan forces led by Callicratidus had severely defeated the Greek navy. Athens was obliged to send relief ships, and every able-bodied sailor, trained or not, was immediately needed on the high seas. Before noon, 150 boats set sail. Hercules and Lippos stood together aboard the trireme, constructed so hastily that it had not yet been given a name. The ship was filled with 140 rowers. They sat on three levels, 23 oarsmen at each level on each side of the boat. One coxswain and a relief coxswain brought the total to 140 men on the rowing decks. Just above was where the 20 marines and their servants stood. Above that was the top deck, forbidden to all but the captain, boatswain, and a few other selected officers.

The marine quarters were bearable. When Lippos grumbled about the lack of seating, Hercules took a knee. "Sit here."

Lippos was surprised at how comfortable a chair could be made from a hyper-muscled leg. The bone was beneath many layers of leg muscles. The fleet had hoped to reach the islands by sundown, but they only made the tip of the Athenian peninsula at Sounion. The rowers carried the relatively light ship ashore while the marines and officers filled the rowboats.

Hercules and Lippos made camp nearby but away from the crowd. They unrolled their blankets and watched the constellations make their way across the night sky.

"That's Orion's Belt. See?" Lippos pointed to the three stars to the north.

"What's underneath his belt?"

"You mean Orion's Sword?"

"Yes," said Hercules, "His sword." He reached under and put a meaty paw at the base of Lippos's enormous cock.

An hour later, Lippos rolled off Hercules, his flesh sword withdrawing from the hole between the powerful glutes. As it slithered out, Hercules shivered with deep pleasure. Lippos licked the sweat that had pooled in the hollow of Hercules's butt. When the boy's heavy cock-head hit the blanket with a "thunk," Hercules let out a silent fart to release the air Lippos had pounded into him. The silence was interrupted by a gurgling sound as Lippos's semen joined the air being expelled. Hercules giggled childishly at his own wet fart.

As they lay arm in arm under the stars, Hercules asked, "Where did you learn astrology?"

Lippos replied. "In the royal courtyard in Larissa."

"Are you an Aeolian?"

"We prefer to call ourselves Thessalonians," said Lippos.

Hercules said, "I hear Thessaly is beautiful."

"It is. We have snowy mountains, sandy beaches, meadows, forests and grasslands. The sun rises over the Magnesian hills and sets behind Mount Titanus. On a clear day, we can see Mount Olympus from the palace."

Hercules kissed his lover. "Someday, we shall go there together. Your parents will be astonished by the man you've become."

It was true. Between the training and the sips of sweat, Lippos had grown from a scrawny boy to a rapidly thickening, virile man. He had sprouted a dark beard, which only served to frame his beauty and masculinity.

Lippos turned away. "My father, King Amyntor, is

ashamed of me. He says I am deformed and an embarrassment. Word spread through the palace, and I was sent to Piraeus to die in the navy."

Hercules frowned. "Deformed? Not in my eyes. King Amyntor bears the same curse?"

Lippos shook his head. "There was a bard in Larissa who bore my same curse. The King calls me his son, but rumors say otherwise. That is the real scandal that sent me away. Mother was banished to a cell deep below the palace. I cry for her every day."

Hercules wiped a tear from that beautiful face. "How did the king know?"

Lippos shrugged. "As a child, I kept my cock hidden, bound in tight linen. I insisted on bathing alone. But a few years ago, Basiliskos, a new servant, barged in on me while I was drying from my bath. I begged him for discretion, but I know he told the king."

"And so your father sent you into my arms."

"The king did, yes. My father wasn't so lucky. The servants told me the royal court raised a scaffold and performed a public hanging in the amphitheater of the bard. They told me my father was stripped naked, so all could see his deformity."

Hercules frowned. "It's not a deformity. Your cock is beautiful." He hugged the youth tightly to his enormous chest. Lippos fell asleep among the blond curly chest hairs.

HUNGRY HOLE

At dawn, the sailors returned their ship to the sea. They were behind schedule and needed to row for many long hours to reach Andros. They had hoped to reach Kios the day before, but the rocky waters made it impossible to reach the island. They needed to reach Andros today, so they took the straits and headed northeast. A storm blew in, but the ship was built to withstand a gale, so it only caused a slight seasickness. Hercules held tight to Lippos as he vomited.

The storm retreated, and the afternoon light glowed golden off the waters of the Aegean. Night fell, but after a worrisome hour, the lighthouse at Gavrio at last appeared on the horizon. Within an hour, the fleet of 150 ships beached along the sandy shores.

As the amorous couple searched for a private cove to make camp, they ran into Thraxos, the muscular boatswain. He extended his arm, and Hercules encircled it with his mighty paw.

"Khaire, Hercules!"

"Kairos dei," said Hercules. It was a joke. Although they had seen each other two days prior, Hercules had offered "long time, no see" as his greeting. The two buffed men chuckled.

"Is this the same weak, skinny Lippos conscripted to Kratos the ugly?"

"The very same!" Lippos smiled as he took Thraxos's forearm in his hand.

"But you're so strong! I've never seen someone leave basic training as changed as you are! And we were interrupted, so you never finished!"

Lippos shrugged. He had a secret elixir and felt it best to leave it private.

Unlike Hercules, whose chest, arms, and legs sprouted a soft layer of blond hairs, Thraxos was utterly smooth. His entire body was hairless as marble. With his tiny penis, he was the true ideal of male beauty. As Hercules looked the man up and down, Lippos felt himself stiffen.

Thraxos said, "Man, I long for something like what you two have with each other. I've always been alone."

Hercules, who never minced words, said, "Surely, with that striking face and that incredible body of yours, you have been with many men." He put one hand on the man's sizable rump.

"Many visitors, no long-term guests." Again, the two shared a laugh. Lippos joined in.

Thraxos leaned in as though the sea itself could overhear him. "I have a confession. I don't mind my tiny penis, but I don't like the small ones up here." He put a hand over his rump. "In fact, I can only enjoy it when it's so big it hurts."

Lippos had spread out the blankets and left the two men to flirt. He wasn't jealous. He knew Hercules was his and his alone. But he could be shared with the right man. Thraxos seemed like a good prospect. He would never be able to take Lippos, but he might enjoy Hercules's massive pole.

Hercules called to Lippos.

"What is it, Hercules?"

"Thraxos here says he is able to take any size, even you. Do you believe him?"

Lippos shook his head.

Thraxos became more interested. "I only ever saw it out of the corner of my eye. I doubted what I had seen. Is it true?"

Lippos nodded. This whole time, he thought Hercules would end up with Thraxos, but this was different.

"May I see it?"

Lippos shrugged and raised his toga just a few inches to reveal the tip banging against his shin.

Thraxos gasped. "That's incredible! Let me see the whole thing."

Lippos was not used to being treated like a prize pony. Most men were disgusted by his monstrous appendage. He raised the toga to his waist, revealing the entire length and thickness of his soft penis.

Hercules said, "See, I told you."

Then Thraxos revealed the bizarre plans he and Hercules had devised. "So, Lippos first, then, once I am accustomed, you will enter me too."

Thraxos put his head on the blanket and thrust his rump skyward. It was so smooth and hairless that Lippos was compelled to rub the glossy cheeks. Lippos put shortening on his cock as it grew and hardened. He lay on his back while Thraxos pushed his way back onto him until the head popped past his sphincter. As the muscular boatswain continued to push back, his smooth legs shined in the moonlight. As Lippos filled him, Thraxos moaned softly. He was close enough to Lippos that the boy could caress his smooth chest and pinch his meaty nipples. Thraxos's tiny cock, not much bigger than a pinky, dribbled fluid from the pressure against his prostate gland.

"We're halfway there," Lippos said as the massive cockhead popped past the colorectal junction. Thraxos shivered with delight. Lippos pushed his way to the end of the sigmoid colon, where he bumped into a wall. Just as with Hercules, any pressure against that wall, which was the edge of the descending colon, caused Thraxos to howl with ecstasy.

"Oh shit, I never felt a man there before. Oh, Zeus and all his children! Oh gods!"

Lippos smiled. He felt powerful, reducing this body-builder to a pile of moaning flesh.

Thraxos used his legs to raise and lower himself a few dozen times, causing both men to grow intoxicated by sex. Lippos liked muscular men, the way they endured pain, and turned it into pleasure.

"Hercules, it's your turn. Come join us."

Lippos thought they would split the man in two. Hercules didn't fit. He pushed hard multiple times, but the fat cockhead couldn't get inside the hole that was so completely stuffed with Lippos's magnificent cock. Thraxos reached behind himself and grabbed hold of the thick log of flesh belonging to Hercules.

"One, two, three! Push!" As Hercules pushed, Thraxos pulled until suddenly, there was a loud pop as the cockhead found its way inside the man. The pressure against the base of Lippos's cock felt better than sex. As Hercules wriggled his fat cock deeper, it caused Lippos to spasm.

"Oh Gods! That feels so good." Lippos wasn't sure if he had said that aloud or if Thraxos had. Hercules was still applying tremendous force to push past the colorectal valve. When he did, it made a loud slapping noise.

Thraxos leaned forward and kissed the blanket. As Hercules forced the last few inches inside him, Thraxos shot out a load of semen from his tiny prick. He hadn't even touched himself. Hercules began to thrust, which did two things. First, it brought forth another hands-free orgasm from the muscled boatswain. Second, it made Lippos want to come. He thought being inside Hercules was the closest he could feel, but tonight, he felt even closer as together they destroyed this man's hole. Hercules was kneeling atop Lippos, who was stretched out on the blanket. Lippos reached up and licked the furry balls of his lover.

"Oh, man! Do it!" While Lippos slurped on Hercules's balls, he continued to caress the smooth chest of Thraxos. Every time he pinched a nipple, the man shot a load of semen. It was like milking a cow, only the milk didn't come from the teat.

Lippos couldn't thrust much from his position on the ground. Hercules sensed his frustration and lay back, pushing Lippos aside so he could twist and get to his knees. Of course, with his penis buried deep inside Thraxos, it wriggled and twisted to accommodate the new position. More semen shot from the tiny penis.

Now Lippos was the one thrusting past Hercules. He pulled out and pushed back in, using the head of his cock to stimulate the shaft of his lover. Hercules bucked like a mule. Thraxos said nothing. His eyes fluttered as they rolled back.

"I'll never feel full enough again," he wailed. "You're so thick and so long, both of you! "

Hercules lifted his head and kissed his lover. Lippos, unprepared for the loving gesture, took a moment to reciprocate. Soon, their tongues were as intertwined as their two cocks were inside Thraxos, the muscle man. It created a sort of circuit - the two tongues and two cocks connecting the men in shared bliss.

Climax would come for both simultaneously. Lippos licked the sweat from Hercules's brow, which gave him a head rush. Hercules could feel Lippos grow impossibly thick inside the hole they shared. That thickness, Hercules knew, was a signal that Lippos would soon be filling Thraxos with warm white come. Just thinking about it put Hercules over the top.

"I'm gonna come!" Hercules grabbed Thraxos by the waist to pull him close.

Lippos said, "Me too. I'm there."

Thraxos, who could scarcely form a sentence since this had started, said, "Fill me up."

The floodgates opened for both men. An impossibly large volume of semen splattered Thraxos's guts. As more and more of the hot sticky come spewed from the two cocks, Thraxos reached orgasm for the fifth time. It was his biggest load yet.

Still stuffed with cock, Thraxos farted loudly. With the fart came a torrent of come that soiled the blanket.

Thraxos stood slowly. First Hercules, then Lippos fell from inside him. Another blanket-staining river of semen gushed out of his loose, flappy hole. It was so loose now, it had lips like a vagina. When he pushed the last bit of come out, his bright red rectum turned inside out, revealing a lump that looked like a bright red sea creature. As quickly as it had emerged, it popped back inside past the grey lips that lined his gaping sphincter. Hercules slapped the man's ass; it contracted even further.

Exhausted from a long day and intense sex, the three sailors fell asleep, the boatswain and the servant nestled in the arms of Hercules, whose pectoral muscles made a perfect pillow for their weary heads.

❧ 6 ❧

SIREN SONG

The sailors had to rise before dawn. The island of Lesbos, where the distress call originated, was many leagues north northeast of Andros. They would have to cross vast open seas with no known islands between them. They planned a very long day, but they could never have foreseen how it would turn out.

In the very middle of the Aegean Sea, leagues away from any known island, a speck appeared on the horizon. Within minutes, it became clear that the Spartan navy was on the warpath, headed right for them. The scout determined there were 120 Spartan ships against their 150 Athenian vessels. Odds were in their favor, but given the bloodthirsty reputation of the Spartans, it seemed more like an even match. But they had a wild card in their midst: the demigod Hercules. He couldn't shoot an arrow to save his life, but the enemy's arrows bounced off his tight, muscled skin. His spear-throwing was powerful but poorly aimed. He needed to find a weapon that capitalized on his brute strength. It turned out he was the weapon.

Among the ships in the Athenian fleet were the rams - designed to strike a warship broadside and cleave it in two. Of course, the Spartans had several as well.

When a ram came heading straight for the ship where Hercules and Lippos were standing, the muscle man ran to the middle of the boat to meet the ram. Before the vessel could strike, Hercules lifted and twirled it, sending all the occupants into the watery depths. For even greater effect, Hercules jumped into the sea and destroyed the remaining Spartan ram ships with his bare hands.

Every Spartan arrow was aimed at this terrifying man with the strength to crush ships with his bare hands. He grabbed an Athenian ram and plowed it into the boat that held Callicratidus, the feared leader of the Spartan military. The Spartan ship cleaved in two, and the Athenian ram suffered barely a scratch.

Spartans were like bees. With their leader lost to the sea, they grew angry. They fought wildly and ferociously. Many Athenians lost their life. Hercules made his way through the water to several dozen Spartan ships, all of which he smashed into bits. One drowning Spartan, desperate to see victory, pulled his sword and swung at Hercules. He laughed, catching the sword in his bare hand, tossing it to catch the handle, and beheading the man, sending him to his watery grave.

To the surprise of every sailor, the Athenian fleet that had initially sent out the distress signal came limping into battle. The Greek commander eventually learned that the twenty-two Athenian boats that remained after their defeat had been held hostage, and the distress signal was meant to lure the entire Greek fleet to Spartan waters. It backfired because the captive Greek vessels overpowered the remaining Spartans and escaped to join the battle.

The sun had just touched the horizon when the last Spartan vessels surrendered. There were no islands or lighthouses to help the Greeks find their way. They had to settle down for the night on the open waters. Hercules and Lippos curled up in a corner and slept. When they woke, the ship was empty. A strange fog enveloped them. There were no other ships in sight.

Lippos asked, "Are we in the underworld? Did we die?"

Hercules shook his head. Hauling Lippos piggyback style, he jumped into the waters. Hercules thought they would find another ship, but theirs was all alone. Then they heard a peculiar sound. It started as a whistle and ended with a shriek.

"Sirens!" Lippos said. "Why didn't they take us?"

Hercules shrugged. "I'm not into women. Neither are you. Maybe we're immune."

It appeared they were, for no matter how loud the calls got, neither man went mad. The fog lifted, revealing a tiny uncharted island on the horizon. The two men jumped ship and swam. Using his powerful legs, Hercules propelled them there at a rapid clip. The two lovers collapsed on the tiny beach. They could hear fresh water falling in the center of the island. They heard birds calling. So there was water and likely food as well. The sun grew blisteringly hot, so the two weary sailors crawled into the dense underbrush to wait out the heat in the shade. Hercules caught a snake and skinned it. Lippos started a fire, then gathered water in his helmet, which he had kept throughout this terrible journey.

While filling his helmet, Lippos saw movement in a dark corner of the forest. They weren't alone. It resembled a man. The boy rushed back to Hercules, who had built a spit roast for the snake.

"There's someone here." Lippos widened his eyes in terror.

"Is he hungry? Tell him to come eat!"

The nearby crack of a branch told them there was no need to seek out this man. He emerged naked from the forest. His face resembled a horse's. So did his cock.

"Care to join us?" Hercules smiled and held up the

helmet of water. The man came forward and touched Hercules on the cheek. He jumped back, muttering.

"I can't hear you, fine sir!" Hercules smiled broadly, which caused the man to grin back.

The man said, "I'm sorry, it's been so long since I saw another human; I forgot how to speak."

Lippos leaned forward. "Where are we?"

The man shrugged. "King Amyntor of Larissa banished me here. I have no idea where this is."

Lippos marveled at the man's prodigious cock, which rivaled his own in length and girth. Hercules, too, licked his lips in wonder. He turned to Lippos. "Show him yours."

Lippos blushed but obliged. The man wept. "Where are you from?"

"Larissa."

"Forgive me, my name is Kallios. Is your mother, by chance, Phaedra, the queen?"

Lippos nodded. "She likes her men big like you."

"I loved your mother. I was sent away when my son's endowment was discovered."

"Father?" Lippos was astonished.

Kallios nodded. "You are my son."

Hercules watched in wonder as the two learned of their relationship.

"My father, or rather, the king, told me that you were hanged in the amphitheater."

"The King is not a great man, but he is good. He loved my music. He sent me here with my harp and told me to write songs for the rest of my life. One day, he would come to hear them."

Hercules was dick-crazed. He wanted father and son inside him, fighting to reach the magic place that caused Hercules to tremble. But this reunion was long overdue. He couldn't come between them. But then again, if he let them both inside him, was that between them or around them? The two were just looking at one another now, no talking. Lippos brushed his father's cheek and kissed him. Kallios returned the kiss. Then they fell into silence again.

Hercules threw caution to the wind. "So, Kallios, how long has it been since you've lain with another?"

Kallios turned to Hercules. "I don't know. I lost count of the days."

Lippos knew where Hercules was going. He also knew that he couldn't stop him.

"I let your son penetrate me every night. Would you like a turn?"

Lippos, not wanting to be left out, said, "Only if I can join him."

Hercules smiled broadly. "I think I saw some aloe nearby. We may need it."

It took a whole aloe plant to lubricate father and son. Hercules hand squeezed a batch for himself and applied it liberally to his hole.

Lippos went first. He pushed his way in with minimal effort, then proceeded to fill Hercules. The father lay beneath Hercules. Once his son was buried to the root, he pressed his way in behind him. The father and son shivered as their two giant cocks slid past one another. Lippos grew thicker, as did his father. For the first time since Lippos had been with him, Hercules betrayed a little pain. It was soon gone. Lippos pumped back and forth, causing his father to tremble from the sensation of their cocks rubbing together. They synchronized so that as his father lowered his hips and partially retreated from Hercules, Lippos would push in and the reverse. This mechanical symphony of flesh caused a storm of ecstasy. Hercules saw only the insides of his upper eyelids. He moaned like a goat.

Kallios, deprived of human comfort for so long, whimpered.

Lippos spoke softly. "Yes. You like a daddy and son inside you, don't you."

Hercules moaned louder. "Ohhh, yes!"

"You like that big daddy dick in your butt? You like his son in there with him?"

Because they were taking turns, the sensitive place in Hercules' colon got pounded in double time. He could barely hear now and was blind with his eyes turned upwards. His lashes fluttered in delight.

"Oh, Daddy, oh Lippos, oh gods and goddesses." Hercules hardly knew what he was saying.

The synchronized pumping gathered speed and intensity. Hercules made noises no human could have made. He sang, cried, and laughed.

Kallios said, "Son, I'm going to come in your friend."

Lippos smiled. "Me too."

The father said, "Very soon."

Lippos nodded. They took their pumping to maximum speed. The father was first. He unleashed a torrent of come that had been gathering for years. Lippos felt his father's wet, hot load blow back through the clogged digestive tract. He lost it.

"I'm coming, Dad!" His father slapped him on the ass to encourage him. His true father's hands on his backside was what put him over. He let out a load with nowhere to go. Hercules was full of cock and come, so each new burst spurted out of his ass, landing on Kallios. Lippos licked Hercules behind the ear near his neck, where a large puddle of sweat had formed. It made him come again. Soon, his father was thoroughly covered in the mixture of his son's and his own come.

Hercules rarely felt pain, but this double invasion had given him a real stretch, and it hurt a little. Father and Son softened, and Hercules squeezed out the two giant cocks at once. The sudden emptiness caused him to cramp. As he farted out more come, he twitched and spasmed, feeling an orgasm in his ass. The come gushing out felt like he was ejaculating. It was sublime.

The snake had burnt, but it was still edible. They hungrily devoured their first meal of the day.

The sun set, and Kallios took the two lovers to his home. He had built it over many years. It looked like a squalid hut from the outside, but inside, it was cozy. "I'll put on some clothes."

While their host dressed, Hercules bent over and asked Lippos what he saw.

"I see a beautiful ass."

Hercules spread his cheeks. "Do I have vagina lips like Thraxos?"

Lippos laughed. "No. You're a little loose, but I'm sure it will tighten up by dawn,"

DESERT ISLAND

At daybreak, Kallios prepared a light breakfast and hard-boiled eggs. He boiled herbs for their morning tea. Over the breakfast table, Hercules started planning.

"Kallios, is this place enchanted? Why have you never left?"

"Where would I go?"

"Anywhere. Athens. Larissa. Wherever your songs take you."

Kallios smiled. "I can build a cabin from logs, but I don't have any tools to craft a boat."

Lippos said, "You don't need tools if you have Hercules."

They decided a monoxylon, a simple type of canoe, would be the fastest and most efficient. Hercules would build the boat while father and son built the oars. Using a sharp rock and a large fallen tree, Hercules began to dig out the inside of the canoe. Meanwhile, father and son sought thin, strong rocks to tie to the long branches. They used a crude knife to carve the handles and put a notch in each branch to wedge the blade before tying it. Kallios had plenty of rope and twine since spinning fibers had been an excellent way to pass the time over the years. They wound twine at the handles and used it to fix the blade in place. In case it was needed, they built a third oar to keep inside the boat.

Hercules finished the dugout, then split wood to form three benches. Next to the center bench, he carefully punched two oar-holes. Lippos and his father approached carrying three oars. Hercules was impressed that they had thought of such a contingency. What would you do in the middle of the sea with one oar?

While Hercules rested, Kallios and Lippos walked around the tiny island.

"How is your mother doing?"

Lippos shook his head. "I don't know. I haven't seen her for years."

Kallios grew pale. "Did they kill her?"

"No, they locked her away in a deep dungeon. I was allowed to see her on the Solstice and the Equinox. She is unhappy, of course, but she is alive. She tells me her heart has broken since she learned of your hanging."

"We must go to her. We must show her I am still alive!"

Lippos wore a worried expression. "It's far too dangerous. If we are caught, he might not be so kind to us this time."

Kallios nodded. He had something else on his mind.

"What are you thinking, father?"

The man blushed. "It's awfully silly. I'm embarrassed to say it."

Lippos took his father's hand. "Tell me anything. Ask me anything."

Kallios bit his lower lip. "Okay, I'll just say it to get it out. All my life, I have been fucking men and women with this thing. I have always wanted to know how it feels to be fucked by someone as big as me."

Lippos nodded. "I'll fuck you. Only if you'll fuck me back."

After generous amounts of aloe were applied, Kallios bent over until his shoulder rested against a tree. Lippos was excited to fuck his father. There was something primal and deep about it. He was even more excited about letting his father fuck him.

"Push out and spread your cheeks."

Kallios stretched the hole wide open. Applying saliva to his knob, Lippos pressed against his father's sphincter.

"Go ahead." Kallios stretched his cheeks wide apart.

"Are you sure?"

His father nodded. In one swift movement, Lippos popped his enormous cock head into the hole.

Kallios let out a cry of agony. "Aaagh! Wait there, just wait there, please. It burns."

Lippos waited patiently until his father gave him the go-ahead. He pushed past the inner ring and filled his father's rectum. His father cried in pain but nodded. Lippos pushed through the second hole that led to the sigmoid colon.

"Oh great gods, that feels so good." Lippos needed no more encouragement. He pumped several times to loosen the inner hole and then plowed forward until he hit the descending colon. He was in completely.

"How much more?" His dad panted from pain and ecstasy.

"That's it. All filled up."

Kallios smiled. "Then fuck me hard!"

The moans and cries coming from his father only made Lippos want to fuck him harder. He had uncovered some rage at being cursed with this dick, and fucking his father was helping to dissipate the emotions. He fucked his father harder than he had ever fucked Hercules. Hearing his father moan and beg for more made him dizzy with delight. His father had returned to muttering like he had done the day before when they first met.

"Dad, am I hurting you?"

His father shook his head. Lippos felt more disappointment than relief. He fucked harder still, drawing a little blood and sending his father into spasms of pain and joy.

"Oh shit, kid. It feels so fucking great. Oh Zeus, Oh Athena!"

Lippos smiled. He hoped his father would make him feel good when they switched positions.

"come inside me boy. Spew your baby gravy up my ass."

The dirty talk excited Lippos. His cock gained in girth. His father squealed. Whether it was pain or delight didn't seem to matter.

"I'm gonna come in you, Dad."

"come in me."

Lippos pounded at a breakneck pace, taking extra-long strokes so he pulled past the junction before pushing back in. That felt like lips on his cock, something only Hercules had ever been able to do. Just thinking of Hercules giving him head made him grow to his thickest girth. He could feel his cock turning a corner and stretching the descending colon. That spot made his father emit clear rivers of clear seminal fluid. Seeing his father dribble out his cockhead was the tipping point for him.

"Dad, I'm coming."

"Give it to me, son. I need your come."

With one last thrust, Lippos rounded that corner deep in the colon and sprayed upwards. He could feel the come land on his cock head.

"Oh god, it's so deep. I feel it so deep." Kallios hugged the tree and waited for the shower of come to end.

Eventually, it ended. Lippos stayed buried inside his father until he grew soft. His father couldn't push him out - he was buried too deep. Gently, Lippos removed his penis from the deepest recesses of his father's colon. At that point, peristalsis took charge, ejecting Lippos rapidly from Kallios. His father's ass was bright red, loose as a coin purse. Then came the river. In torrents, Lippos's come poured out of the hole, landing in the soil at the foot of the tree. Just when Kallios thought no more could come, another wave of jism poured out of him. Then, a trickle of blood, nothing serious.

"Okay, my turn." Kallios gave an evil grin that frightened Lippos. He forgot he would have to endure the same thing, roughly, that his father had; it would hurt.

Kallios staggered to his feet. He reeled, then leaned on his son for balance.

"Son, this is going to be on the ground. I must be on my knees."

Lippos lay face down in the grass. His father knelt over him and pressed his immense cock into him. Hercules was thick, perhaps thicker than Kallios. Lippos took his father easily.

"You've done this before, son."

"Yes, sir." Lippos wriggled his butt to encourage his father to go deeper.

The moment his father pushed past the rectum, Lippos moaned aloud. The impossibly long cock, very much like his own, snaked and burrowed deeper into Lippos. At some point, it went further than Hercules could go. And then, it reached the end of the sigmoid colon. Lippos writhed and moaned. He'd never felt so full.

But the noises caused Kallios to thicken in response, and Lippos felt his insides stretched to their limit.

"Oh, Dad, you're so fucking huge." Kallios, bloated and buried deep, thrust his hips back and forth, slowly at first, then faster and faster still. His thrust pushed his son forward in the grass, so Kallios held his legs. Lippos wanted to crawl away from the pain, but the pleasure was so much more intense. He gathered his strength and pushed back into his father's crotch. The effect was paralyzing. He felt his father creeping up his descending colon.

"Are you alright, son?"

Lippos replied, "Shut up and fuck me, Daddy."

Kallios obliged. He found his rhythm and fucked his son into the ground. He came suddenly, his cock growing its thickest. Lippos felt his dad inflating his bowels and filling them with his seed. He feared he would burst apart, but his bowels held. His father pulled out quickly, causing Lippos to cramp. His anus flapped in the breeze as he pushed the come out. It trickled down his balls and into the grass. He felt his father's arms around his middle, hauling him to his feet. The two men held each other tight. Kallios kissed his son on the forehead.

"Son, now we both know how it feels and what our cocks can do to others." They walked slowly, each feeling the bittersweet pain that comes after sex with a big cock. Hercules smiled when he saw them.

"I know what you two must have been doing."

They grinned sheepishly.

Hercules added, "Now you know how it feels." It was true.

A GROWING BOY

Stranded somewhere in the middle of the Aegean, with no compass save for Polaris the North Star, the prospect of setting out in a handmade canoe was pure folly. But Hercules was bound to be a powerful rower, and Lippos knew the stars better than anyone, so they had hope. The plan was to go west. Athens was in the southwest, but anything south would be a longer haul and bore the risk of missing the peninsula, sending them into the Cyclades.

At sunset, the North Star became visible. The three men loaded the boat with crocks of water and the fruit that grew everywhere on the island. When it was full, they hopped into the canoe and set out on their perilous journey. Hercules had never rowed, but he quickly figured out the rhythm and strokes that propelled them at top speed. Lippos marveled at his lover's powerful back muscles. Kallios was stunned by his arms and chest. They rowed all night, then slept in the bottom of the boat. Lippos and his father slept on each arm, their heads nestled in the rower's musky armpits. Lippos licked the sweaty arms and immediately felt new chest hairs sprouting. He also felt his arms grow in girth and strength. When he awoke, he was surprised to stroke his chin and find a beard growing there.

"Hercules, I need to tell you something."

The muscle man leaned in so Lippos could whisper in his ear. 'What is it, brother?"

"You see this?" Lippos stroked his beard.

Hercules nodded.

"That wasn't there last night."

Hercules smiled. "You're growing into a man!"

Lippos said, "It doesn't happen in one night. You have some kind of power, Hercules."

Hercules frowned. "Uh, I don't follow."

Lippos said, "Do you look like your father?"

"No, but I have my mother's eyes." He batted his eyelashes at Lippos.

"I think your father may be from Olympus."

"Why on earth would you think that?" Hercules was bristling with anger.

Lippos spoke plainly. "I grew body hair and muscles from licking your sweat. You must be a child of the gods. Think about your strength and invulnerability."

Hercules grew pensive. "Are you sure this is unrelated to your discovery of a different father?"

"I am certain it is related because that is how I got the idea."

Hercules laughed. "I will have to ask my mother if she screwed around with Zeus."

"I think she may have." They both laughed.

Strong winds sent the canoe drifting in some unknown direction. It rained hard. All three men bailed out the boat with whatever tools they had at hand. As suddenly as the cloudburst began, the dark clouds parted, and the sun shone high above the western horizon. Even though the North Star was the best tool, the setting sun, given the time of the year, was another compass pointing west. So they set out in the direction of the sun. In the evening, the North Star appeared in an unexpected place. It seemed they had traveled northwest. Luckily, there were many inhabited islands in that direction. It was also the path to Thessaly. They came across an island with a natural cove in the middle of the night. Hercules could have kept going endlessly, but Kallios and Lippos needed a break. They made camp on the pebbly beach.

TEMPLE OF DELIGHTS

The island was inhabited. In the morning, they were awoken by a beautiful young man with curly locks of red hair and freckles. The three men offered their hands and their names.

"My name is Eruthros. Welcome to Skiros. Follow me." The redhead swayed his hips as he walked up the trail with the three travelers in tow. His swinging round bottom was hypnotic. By the time they reached the village, all three men had hard-ons that made tents of their tunics.

A large temple dominated the town square. The streets were filled with men who eyed them hungrily.

Lippos whispered, "I think they're going to eat us."

Eruthros tittered. "Don't worry, we're not cannibals."

One by one, the men turned and filed into the temple.

Eruthros gestured. "Go on. You won't be disappointed."

Kallios turned to his son. "Why are there no women?"

Their redhead host said, "Women live on a nearby island. We get together on full moons to procreate with them but prefer to live separately."

Hercules smirked. "What do you do the rest of the time?"

"Come into the temple, and you'll see."

The three visitors followed Eruthros into the stone temple. The lighting was poor. Only a few candles and the light from the entrance broke through the darkness. Alcoves were carved into the stone walls. They created a specialized sort of bench that was meant for sex. Every man in the temple lay in an alcove on his back. Their feet were held aloft in leather stirrups strapped to the wall. Like Eruthros, the men all had big bottoms. Eruthros guided the men into the orgy to come.

"You must try to hold your seed until you have been with every one of us. That is the only rule."

A panpipe sounded softly in the darkness, accompanied by a drum, setting the tone and tempo for the sex that was to come.

Hercules went first. It was logical that the least huge of the three cocks should pave the way for the others. The first man was a short, stocky carpenter with a muscular physique sculpted by many hours of hammering and sawing. Hercules took a wide stance before the man and roughly pushed his way in. The man was experienced. He took the brutal cock without too much resistance. Hercules was mindful of his powerful thrusts, just gently tapping the end of the rectum. The man leaned to one side, and Hercules slipped into the colon. It was going to be hard to hold his load. His cock kept sliding past the junction, in and out, and it felt too good. But the man pushed him away. Hercules moved on to the next man, a fisherman with rough hands but a soft bottom. Lippos knew he was slightly smaller than his father, so he went next. The carpenter's eyes widened when Lippos held his monstrous cock aloft. But he didn't balk. Slowly, tenderly, Lippos positioned his enormous cock head against the hole and pushed his way into the man's ass. He was surprised at how easily he entered him. It was enough of a turn-on that he thickened a little. The man made his first sound - a grunt of pleasure. When Hercules finished with the fisherman, the carpenter pushed Lippos away and welcomed Kallios. The trio continued the ceremony until every last man had been thoroughly fucked but not bred. They managed to keep their cool and didn't spill their seed inside anyone.

Eruthros, who was in one of the alcoves, said, "Now you must select a favorite to receive your come."

Both Kallios and Lippos liked the very first man, the carpenter. Hercules was horny for their host, Eruthros. He stood before the boy and pounded him silly. After having the other two cocks, Hercules seemed easy, if not a bit thicker. Eruthros moaned in delight when Hercules pushed past the rectum.

Kallios and Lippos were in a quandary until the carpenter pulled on both of their cocks. He gestured for them both to fuck him at once. Eruthros was the only man on the island who spoke the Athenian dialect, so sex was nonverbal, with only groans, grunts, fingers, and sighs to punctuate the silent effort.

Lippos went first. He lay in the alcove beneath the man, penetrating him from below. The carpenter groaned loudly. He let Lippos dig and burrow his way to the end of his sigmoid colon, grunting with pleasure. With Lippos most of the way in, Kallios stepped up and spread his legs apart, standing on tiptoe to reach the elevated hole, which was already stuffed and stretched. Like magic, he entered the carpenter, stuffing him beyond capacity. Now, the groans were genuine. He was in pain. But it didn't matter; he pulled the daddy closer, forcing him inside. Lippos moaned, loving that new feeling of his father's massive cock sliding against his own colossal tool.

Meanwhile, Hercules had found the sweet spot that tickled his cock head and sent Eruthros into fits of ecstasy. "Oh, Hercules, you're so powerful. Oh god, you're so thick and powerful." The redhead stroked the rippling muscles.

Hercules concentrated on tickling his penis just right. He wanted to give this hot man the load of come he deserved.

Kallios and Lippos pumped in and out of the carpenter as they had done with Hercules - one in while the other out, then vice versa. The carpenter blew short bursts of air like a woman giving birth. The sound caused Lippos to swell to full size. The sudden swelling made Kallios swell to his maximum, too. The carpenter shouted with joy and shot his load in his own face. That put Lippos over the edge. He pushed his way all the way in and let his father's strokes bring him to climax. He unleashed a torrent of hot come that suddenly made the carpenter's insides very slippery and warm. Kallios closed his eyes, let out a breath, and added his semen to the already very full asshole. The father and son stayed buried inside their little carpenter until he involuntarily pushed them out. When he expelled their semen, it flew everywhere, spattering their crotch, their cocks, and the temple floor. Then he passed out.

Hercules heard the commotion; it excited him. Eruthros stroked the muscle man's chest, catching a finger on his nipple. This sent shockwaves through Hercules. Eruthros pinched and twisted that nipple, sending Hercules into an intense orgasm. He pounded recklessly, barely aware of the boy's cries of pain. Mercifully, Hercules only lost control for 30 seconds of orgasm before he remembered and turned off the pounding. Eruthros stopped screaming and moaned in pleasure. Hercules pulled out of him quickly, making the boy snap shut with such force he quaked and quivered before farting out the come of Hercules. "Oh, Hercules, I think you hurt me."

Sure enough, blood came out after the come. It kept coming until Eruthros grew pale.

Hercules lifted him and cried out. "Help! Help! He's dying." But blood gushed out of the boy's ass and mouth. He breathed his last breaths.

Every man in the temple was on his feet. They were brandishing weapons and tools of their trades. The fisherman's hook, the carpenter's hammer, and a host of other instruments were drawn and ready to strike.

Kallios and Lippos motioned for Hercules to set the dead youth on the ground.

The three backed out of the temple, followed by the men. Hercules picked up Lippos and Kallios and held them by the waist as he ran down the trail to the beach. He was much faster than the townsfolk. In fear and urgency, they clambered into the canoe.

🎠 10 🎠

HAYRIDE

Hercules rowed with all his might. Once they were a safe distance from shore, they stopped to get their bearings. It was early afternoon, and the sun had not indicated where it would set. For a few hours, they rowed in the direction they had been going when they found the island, but it was hard to keep on course. Not trusting the sun, Lippos waited for the North Star to guide the boat. To his dismay, he saw that they were going north-northwest. He asked Hercules to correct his course, and they rowed all night. Hercules felt deep shame and regret for what he had done. The words of his friend Lippos echoed in his ears. Perhaps his father was a resident of Mount Olympus. Why else would he be so much stronger than anyone else in Greece? Only a god could fuck a man to death.

The boat passed several dark islands in the night. They felt it would be better to find the mainland, where customs were more genteel. At dawn, they came to a stretch of land that looked far too large to be an island. When the sun arose, Kallios and Lippos both gasped.

Hercules said, "What is it?"

Kallios answered. "We're in Thessaly. I know this

coast; it's Magnesia. If we land at Sepia, we can ride to Larissa. It's a two-day journey at most."

Lippos said, "Father, we can't return. You will be killed."

"I doubt anyone would recognize me," said his father.

Hercules spoke. "You will be with me. Nobody will harm you lest they face the wrath of the demigod!" To emphasize his point, he beat his chest. His meaty fists smacking into his broad chest echoed off the Magnesian coast.

By noon, they pulled their canoe into the harbor. Sepia has a distinct dialect, but both Kallios and Lippos were fluent. They learned from a dock worker that a wagon caravan was leaving shortly, carrying seafood, hay, and other Sepian goods to Larissa. Kallios spoke with Magnos, the hay vendor, and negotiated passage with him. Hercules was the bargaining chip. If anything happened to the wagon, he could repair it. If not, he could carry all the hay on foot. He asked the muscleman to demonstrate. Hercules lifted six bales and stacked them on his shoulders as easily as a woman putting on a shawl. They had a ride in a cart full of hay. It didn't get much better for ordinary folk like Hercules or Kallios. Lippos had often traveled by royal carriage. It hadn't been half as comfortable as their hay wagon.

They made their way through the western coastal towns of Magnesia that looked out onto the Pagasaean Gulf. When night fell, they were in Pherae, less than a day's journey from Larissa. The hay merchant found an inn, but the three hitchers had no money. They slept in the cart, which was quite luxurious. They ate apples and feta that Magnos, the merchant, generously gave them. Hercules promised to help him unload at the hay market if needed.

As the three men finished their light supper, they grew both sleepy and horny in equal measure.

"I'll bet you can't take me in your mouth," Kallios boasted.

"What will you wager?"

"I have nothing of value, but I can give my blessing when you marry Lippos."

"Wouldn't you give it anyway?" Hercules asked.

Lippos grinned. "Didn't you want to suck my cock anyway?"

Lippos spoke up. "I won't be left out of this."

"Fine," Hercules said, "you can take me from behind. It will be a spit roast."

Hercules started with Kallios. He needed to concentrate to widen his mouth enough to accept the massive head in his mouth. Kallios gasped. He had never had more than a tongue on the head of his cock. Now he had a whole mouth around his corona.

Once Hercules was sure he wouldn't need to bite down, he stretched his throat to accommodate more of the colossal cock. Even with Kallios in his esophagus, there was still a foot or more of cock left exposed, Hercules wanted to suck him all the way, but he wasn't sure that their physiology would permit it. He took in a heaving chest full of air and rammed the cock down his throat all the way. He felt it in his chest. Kallios groaned and reveled in the sheer wonder of the accomplishment.

Meanwhile, Lippos knelt behind Hercules and shoved his way into the powerful hole. Hercules chuckled as he pictured Lippos and Kallios meeting somewhere in the middle of his gut. It wasn't possible, but it made for a good fantasy. He sighed through his nose as Lippos pushed his way deeper, past the rectum into his gut. Hercules pushed back, letting his ass swallow more and more cock like a greedy pig eating an eel.

Kallios wept with joy. He had never known how it felt to go deep inside the throat. Hercules was an expert cocksucker. He used his throat muscles to massage the shaft of Kallios's cock. Despite the incredible effort required to accommodate such a gargantuan beast, he didn't gag or struggle. All Kallios knew was that he had never felt anything like it, but he hoped he would again.

Lippos massaged Hercules's great globe-shaped buttocks. They were powerful and muscular, with a dimple on each side. He plowed his way in and dragged his way out of the depths of Hercules's intestines. Hercules oozed sweet, sticky effluence. He had two of the largest cocks in Greece inside him. He knew this was one of life's moments you remember until you die. His mouth and throat were stuffed to capacity. He grew aware of a strange tingling in his throat. The soft tissues were no different than a woman's vagina - they were capable of orgasm. The pride of taking the cock so wholly, coupled with the friction, caused his throat to quiver and contract with pleasure. Those contractions squeezed Kallios's cock, moving him closer to orgasm.

Lippos grew aroused and hypnotized by the sight of his own impossibly large cock disappearing into Hercules and then coming back out, over and over. It was then that he noticed the muscleman's half-hard cock dangling down like a cow's udder. He grabbed the base and milked it, causing Hercules to shudder with extreme lust. He let out a loud grunt, the only sound he could make with his mouth and throat full. There was no doubt he was in ecstasy. The precome flowed heavily from his thick cock. Lippos tugged on the big dick and fucked Hercules hard.

Kallios couldn't last much longer. He slowed down his face-fucking, but it was too late. In great gobs, he shot his come in Hercules's throat and mouth. Hercules swallowed every drop.

Meanwhile, Lippos saw beads of sweat forming on those giant globes that engulfed his cock. He leaned down and licked the sweat. It made him come. He filled

Hercules with his semen, still yanking and milking Hercules from below.

When the hot come filled both his holes one after another, Hercules could take no more. He sprayed the hay with his come in ten great bursts.

As the father and son leaned into Hercules's arms, they grew sleepy. Hercules felt come draining from inside him. The hay would be an excellent protein source for the horses!

11

IN THE COURT OF
THE KING

In the morning, Magnos came for the carriage. They were less than a day away from Larissa. The three men enjoyed basking in the sun while the cart rocked gently from side to side on the well-worn road. They were on the Thessaly Plains now. No mountains cast shade on their path.

Lippos said, "Father, aren't you a wanted man in Larissa?"

Kallios said, "King Amyntor would probably behead me if he knew I were in his fair kingdom."

Hercules said, "Not on my watch. I will protect you from anyone who wishes you harm."

Kallios patted Hercules on his bulging triceps. "You are a true friend."

As the late afternoon sun hovered over Mount Titanus, the hay cart entered the gates of Larissa. Hercules assisted the merchant with his bales of hay. A small crowd gathered to marvel at the muscular haybale making quick work of a whole cart. The three men thanked Magnos and took off walking down the high street. The townspeople smiled and beamed at Hercules, who exuded a blond, tan glow of friendliness as he flashed his teeth. Lippos spoke first. "We haven't made a plan. We need to stay at an inn, and we haven't an obol between us."

Kallios said, "Do you have money in your room at the palace?"

Lippos nodded. "I will go greet my father and tell him I am in town for only one day. He still thinks I am in the navy, not a deserter."

Hercules said, "He likely would have received word of your death. Our ship was empty after we jumped. He'll be shocked to see you alive."

Lippos pondered this. "You're right. I need a better story."

Kallios said, "The best approach is for Hercules to bring you to your father and demand a reward for saving your life. You will get much gold."

It was a brilliant plan. At nightfall, Hercules carried Lippos to the palace. The young man pretended to be unconscious. The guards tried to keep them from entering, but Lippos limply raised his head and spoke the name of one of the guards blocking their way, Demetrius.

"Master Lippos, is that you?"

Lippos nodded weakly. "Please, Demetrius, I need to see my father."

The guard snapped his fingers. "Straight away, Master Lippos."

The portcullis was raised. They entered the courtyard.

"His court is on the second floor. Use the right staircase." Lippos spoke in a whisper.

Hercules followed the lad's instructions. When they reached the second floor, they turned left and walked through another guarded doorway. The guards recognized Lippos and stood aside. Sitting at an enormous table was a cruel, brooding man who scarcely merited the crown perched on his gray head. He was deep in his cups. "What is the meaning of this!?"

Hercules took a knee. "Your Highness, I have your son Lippos in my arms."

The king stood up quickly, knocking over a flagon of wine.

"Hello...father...it's...me." Lippos laid his wrist on his forehead, signaling illness.

King Amyntor looked very displeased. But he was not alone at the table. Other members of court were watching the unfolding drama, praying for more scandal. The king knew he had to put on a performance.

"My darling Lippos, I was in mourning. How did you survive the battle?"

Lippos said, "Ask Hercules. He rescued me."

Hercules cleared his throat. "It's true, your highness. He was drowning, and I brought him to a deserted island."

The King nodded. "And how did you get here from there?"

"We built a canoe, your highness. We rowed for two days until we came to an inhabited island, then two more days after that until we landed in Magnesia."

"That battle was near Lesbos. How did you cross the Aegean in a rowboat?"

Lippos spoke. "Hercules is the strongest man in Greece."

Hercules added, "Some say I'm strongest in the world."

Amyntor put his index fingers together before his nose. "Indeed? How can we see a demonstration of your power?"

Hercules said, "I am up for any challenge. Just name the day and place."

Lippos said, "Father, we should reward Hercules for saving my life."

The look on Amyntor's face betrayed his true feelings: he didn't want to reward anyone for foiling his plans. But all eyes were on him; he had to put on a show for the court members.

"I will reward him handsomely when he proves he is the world's strongest man."

They needed money now, not after a pageant. Lippos thought quickly. "I'm too weak to walk. Hercules, please carry me to my bedroom."

When they were alone with the bedroom door shut, Lippos leaped to his feet. "That didn't go well."

Hercules, not the best strategist, had to ask. "What are we going to do?"

Lippos smiled. He knelt below his writing desk. There were blank parchment scrolls stacked underneath. He reached under the parchment and retrieved a leather purse. "Aha! It's still here."

He handed the purse to Hercules.

"This is yours, Lippos."

"Yes, but I'm not going to the inn with you. I have to stay here for appearances."

Hercules understood. "How will I get back in the palace?"

"Send that young guard Demetrius to see me. I'll instruct him to let you in no matter what. We were childhood friends, so he is loyal to me, not the King."

"I've been by your side for months. It will break my heart to leave you here, Lippos."

Lippos nodded. "I, too, will be lonely, but we must rescue my mother for Kallios."

Hercules hung his head, sticking out his lower lip like a baby. Lippos caressed him, hugged him, kissed him, and sent him away to find Kallios and to acquire a room at the inn. Hercules put the leather purse around his neck and left. Lippos lay in his bed to further the illusion of illness.

12

AN OLD FLAME

Demetrius came bounding up the stairs and into Lippos's chamber. "Master Lippos, your handsome friend said you needed me."

Lippos smiled. "Demetrius, you can just call me Lippos. We are friends."

The guard blushed. "Is that why you sent for me?"

Lippos laughed. "No. It's to ask a favor. If my handsome friend returns, even if he is not alone, I need you to let him in. We were in the Navy together and now have many plans to make."

Demetrius grinned. "Lippos, your friend is so handsome. I saw the way he looked at you. You feel more than brotherly love for that man."

"You got me, Demetrius. Hercules is my lover, and I am his. It's an erotic love."

Demetrius grew serious. "My heart breaks. I love you, Lippos. I imagined one day we would live together somewhere far away, where kings and palaces have no meaning."

Lippos brushed away a tear from the guard's face. "Don't be sad, friend. I'm yours right now if you want me."

"No, you couldn't walk. How can we make love?"

Lippos stood and kissed the swarthy guard on the lips. "I'm fine. It was an act."

Demetrius held Lippos by the head and looked into his eyes. "You are sneaky."

Lippos marveled at how his friend had matured. He was tall, with green eyes that sparkled in the candle-light. His chest was broad with protruding nipples that showed through his uniform. His feet were three sandal sizes bigger than Lippos remembered. And the nipples weren't the only body part poking at the tunic.

The kisses grew more passionate. Demetrius pushed Lippos onto the bed and lifted his legs skyward. He crouched and pressed his mustache to his childhood friend's anus. He explored the hole with his tongue. Lippos moaned and spread his butthole. "Demetrius, I missed you."

The guard pulled out a dick that would be considered large by most standards. It was not as big as Hercules and certainly nowhere near the size of the cock of Kallios. Demetrius coated his proud cock in spit and prepared for a tight squeeze. To his astonishment, he slid in with ease. "Damn, Lippos, you're as loose as a sandal!"

Lippos giggled. "I was in the navy. I met a couple of guys."

"Bigger than me?" Demetrius sounded alarmed.

Lippos shrugged. "You feel good inside me. Fuck me."

Demetrius needed no further encouragement. He pushed his way deep, past the rectum. Lippos grunted like a truffle pig. A man's size scarcely mattered as long as he was big enough to push their way past the second hole. The lanky guard watched his cock sliding in and out of Lippos with awe. It was so loose he felt compelled to stroke his cockhead by pushing past the colorectal junction. The young prince's butthole wasn't tight enough to do the trick, but he just kept pushing harder, deeper, faster.

Lippos had loved Demetrius once. This artful fucking was one of the reasons he had fallen for him. His butt cheeks jiggled with each downstroke. Demetrius caressed those cheeks with his calloused hands. He kissed the back of Lippos's neck, which sent shivers down the prince's spine.

Demetrius was young and fast. The shivers were all that was needed to begin that tingling in his balls. "Oh shit, Lippos."

"You close?"

"Yeah. Unnnh!" The tall guard felt his balls contract before letting loose a torrent of come inside Lippos. He pulled out and stuffed his big slab of meat back into his pants. "Damn, Lippos, you have a sweet ass."

"And you're a masterful ass fucker, my dear friend."

Demetrius sighed. "Are you really in love with another?"

Lippos nodded. He flipped over and sat up. "You were my first love, Demetrius. If I ever take power, I will ensure you have a place by our side."

Demetrius smiled. "Young love, first love, it doesn't always survive. But my love and devotion for you will always be there."

Lippos leaned forward. "Speaking of devotion, we need help from you and the other guards."

"Our help? With what?"

"I'm going to rescue my mother from the dungeon."

Demetrius said, "You're asking us to commit treason. I don't want to die."

"We have Hercules. He's an army unto himself. He and my real father will keep you safe."

Demetrius said, "You need to lock us in the dungeon. That way, it will look like we were overpowered and had to hand over the keys."

Lippos kissed Demetrius. "Thank you!"

After Demetrius left, Lippos drifted off into a deep, dreamless slumber.

13

HOT BATH

Hercules met up with Kallios in a dark corner of the market.

"Did he find money?"

Hercules nodded. Kallios had decided on the most inconspicuous inn. It was called "Pandokeia Helix". It was a private inn, unlike the public inn where pilgrims stayed. The innkeeper was an ancient crone with terrible eyesight.

"That's a quarter Obol per night. Includes meals, fresh linens, and use of the bath. We have a hot spring. Smells like farts, but it will get you clean. You both look like you could use a good wash."

The men found their room near the back, close to the bathing area.

"I'm going to take her up on that bath. Care to join me?" Hercules removed his tunic. Kallios shed his clothing, and the two men walked out the back door to the waiting tub.

Vapors rising from the sulfuric waters smelled like bad gas, but the water was rich with minerals. Hercules scrubbed Kallios's back, and then they switched positions. Layers of skin cells and dirt came off, leaving their skin silky soft. They leaned back on opposite sides of the tub, with legs spread. Kallios gazed at the layers of muscle Hercules wore like a cloak. Each time he moved his arm, his nipple would twitch. Without thinking about it, Kallios began to stroke his cock.

Hercules was aware that he was being admired. He liked it. He stroked his cock in response. The two men met in the middle and kissed. Their cocks brushed against each other, swelling rapidly. Hercules rotated and put his hands on the edge of the tub, offering his broad buttocks to Kallios, whose cock had reached its way out of the water and was still growing. Kallios backed up so he could put his cock inside the muscle-man. Hercules didn't flinch. He let out a low growl as Kallios pushed his way in. He could feel the serpentine cock twisting and bending its way further and further up inside him. It felt like he was a sausage casing being stuffed with thick meat. Hercules was happy to serve the father of his lover. He felt no pain; mortal men would scream in agony. He was designed for this.

The water churned as Kallios plunged his way in and out of the massive, accommodating ass.

"Damn, Hercules, you feel so good. My son is so lucky to have you."

"His mother can take you, right?" Hercules wiped the sweat from his brow.

"She can. Not up front, but in the back."

Hercules imagined what it would be like to be Lippos's mother, taking Kallios inside him. He stroked a sweaty, wet nipple as he thought about the two of them. Sometimes, it was hard being a hulking male demigod. Sometimes, he just wanted to be the woman. The harder he pinched his nipple, the more gratified he became. He felt Kallios swell to his maximum, a sure sign he would be coming soon. The father of his lover climaxed deep inside him. A few strokes of his own thick cock brought him to orgasm. He aimed his cock and shot his semen on the stones surrounding the tub. He didn't want to dirty the bath water.

Exhausted and clean, the two men settled into their bed for the night.

❦ 14 ❦
A PLAN

In the morning, Lippos walked to the market to meet Hercules. He was extra cautious, wearing a plain tunic so as not to be distinguished in the crowd. He looked over his shoulder to be sure palace spies were not following him. Kallios did not join them; he stayed in the room to avoid being recognized by anyone who knew him.

"What's the plan, Lippos?"

"I got the guards to agree to a charade. They'll let us lock them in the dungeon, so it looks like we overpowered them before taking Mother. We may need Kallios as a lookout. Is he willing to risk being seen?"

Hercules shrugged. "If he's part of the plan, he'll do what's needed."

Lippos scanned the busy marketplace for spies but saw none. He and Hercules returned to the inn. At the front, the ancient crone said, "No visitors allowed."

Hercules dropped 1/16 of an Obol on her desk. She nodded and let them pass.

Kallios hugged his son when he learned of the plan. "I will keep watch while you free Phaedra from her cell."

Lippos frowned. "Where do we go to escape?"

Hercules tapped his lover on the head. "That's

thinking ahead. We need an escape plan and a destination."

The three men retired to the bath to think. The pungent water and minerals were arousing. Their half-hard cocks floated to the surface as they figured out the plan.

"Do you think Magnos will be back to town?" Lippos asked.

Hercules nodded. "Back home, we harvest hay every 40 days. He'll be back in a few fortnights."

"That's not soon enough. Every day I stay in Larissa, I risk exposure." Kallios thought for a minute, then, "There are carts for sale in the marketplace. I'm sure you saw them."

Lippos nodded. "I did. They're empty, but they are for sale. We have no covering and no oxen to pull them."

Kallios smiled and patted Hercules. "Here is your ox."

Hercules took offense but then laughed, knowing it was true.

"We don't need a full hay cart. Just a sledge big enough to hold me, Phaedra, and Lippos."

Lippos said, "But everyone will recognize Hercules. And us."

"We'll be under blankets, son. Hercules will wear a bearskin to mask his identity."

Hercules said, "The shopping list is one bearskin, two blankets, and one modest sledge."

Next, they needed to decide on a destination.

Kallios said, "It must be far from the influence of Larissa."

Hercules said, "I have always wanted to see Poseidonia on the Italian Peninsula. That's certainly beyond the reach of King Amyntor."

The three agreed it was a suitable destination. The trouble was how far it was from Larissa.

Lippos said, "We can catch a boat in Thessalonika. We can't go to Piraeus, or we'll be hanged as deserters."

Kallios said, "The port of Appolonia is on the Ionian Sea. It's where Thessalians go to ship goods to Magna Graecia. It's many days' walk from here to the Lacmon pass, but once we are over the Pindus, the great river Aous flows there. We can rest on the river journey. Be sure the sledge can be made to float as well."

Lippos looked concerned. "Mother may be in no shape to walk such a distance."

Hercules smiled. "Not to worry, my love. I will carry all three of you since I never tire."

Kallios added, "When you buy your bearskin, stop and buy a peasant woman's dress for Phaedra and shoddy clothes for Lippos, too. I will wear Lippos's robes because they will be looking for a filthy mendicant."

Lippos mourned the loss of his home. In truth, he had been thrown out months ago. But he always believed he would return to stay.

Hercules lifted a powerful hand and brushed away Lippos's tears. "Hey, it's okay. We'll start a new life in Poseidonia."

Lippos kissed the giant paw. "I know, but I will miss my home."

Hercules dried off and took the coin purse to the market. He bought a large sledge and parked it in front of the inn. He returned and searched in vain for a bearskin. Instead, he bought a lion's skin. He also purchased a frumpy dress for Phaedra and a cheap tunic for Lippos. He was nearly out of cash after he bought wool blankets. He wasn't a skilled bargainer.

Lippos grew frightened when he saw their money had run out.

Hercules said, "Can't you ask your father for more?"

"I'm not supposed to have any. That's why I had to hide the coin purse in my room."

Hercules rubbed his chin. "Does your father have a vault?"

"Yes. In the palace basement."

"It's heavily guarded, I assume?"

Lippos shook his head. "It's behind a door which cannot be opened by anyone but the king. The locks are strong. He keeps the keys around his neck."

Hercules flexed a bicep. "Not a problem."

Lippos grew terrified. "If you steal money, they'll chop your head off or worse."

"I'd like to see them try."

Kallios smiled. "We don't need to take it all. Just what Phaedra and my son deserve. Two-thirds perhaps?"

Lippos laughed. "We could never carry so much gold. There is no room in the sledge. One large chest will suffice."

Hercules flexed his chest and winked. Lippos kissed his sweaty pectoral muscles, savoring the masculine scent. He felt his legs grow hairier and his neck thickened when he licked the man's teats. The scraggly beard on his face grew thicker.

Hercules saw the effect his sweat had on the boy. In truth, he was excited to be with a masculine lover, not a pretty young man. It made the violation of his nether regions all the more exciting. Thinking about it, he grew hard, lifting the hem of his tunic high in the air.

Kallios retired to the bath so the two lovers could be alone together.

The warm weather made both men sweat tremendously. Lippos kneeled and licked the sweat from the crack of Hercules's ass. He probed the hole with his tongue, enjoying the coppery taste it left in his mouth. He had wanted to do this since they met.

"Ohhhhh! Ohhhhh!" Hercules liked having his ass eaten. Lippos milked the thick cock hanging down between Hercules's legs as he probed ever deeper with his tongue. His erection grew and lifted off the ground, getting caught under the bed. Clamped to Hercules with his mouth, he slid back to free his meat from the furniture. It rose in pulses until it was within Hercules's field of vision. The muscular hunk leaned forward and took the tip in his mouth. They were in a sixty-nine position now, with Lippos pushing his way past the tonsils with his cock, while probing the prostate gland with his tongue. Hercules gobbled the cock down his throat, loving the feeling of it swelling inside him.

Lippos pulled back and hocked a gob of spit on the muscular hole. He spit several more times, then grabbed Hercules by the legs, raising the meaty thighs skyward. With no warning, he pushed his cock deep into Hercules, who howled with delight. Deep as he was, Lippos was only halfway inside. Hercules could see the exposed flesh waiting to enter him. He nodded, and Lippos pushed past the rectum and filled his colon with throbbing cock.

"Ohh, yeah! Just like that! Right there!" Hercules encouraged Lippos to fuck harder, faster, and deeper. "All the way, man, fill me up! Hurry and fill me up! It doesn't hurt; don't hold back."

Lippos had no intention of holding back. With this latest sweat-induced growth spurt, he had gained a stronger desire to thrust his groin and rock his hips. It felt powerful to dominate a muscleman like Hercules, making him thrust harder like a rutting dog.

Hercules was excited to have such a masterful lover. He thought of the timid boy who was taunted in the barracks. He bore no resemblance to the virile ass fucker inside him now.

A bead of sweat fell from Lippos into Hercules's mouth. Instantly, Hercules became more passive, begging Lippos to overpower him. A tingling in his belly turned into a series of contractions. He imagined it was what a woman might feel during orgasm. His whole lower digestive tract was like a sensitive, slippery pussy that needed fucking hard. Hercules lost the power of speech entirely. He bucked and tossed, his dripping cock spreading precome all over the blankets. The intestinal orgasm had not abated. Hercules let his eyes roll back in his head while he made sounds one might hear at a livestock exhibition. His butt cheeks squeezed hard against Lippos's cock in an effort to slow him down, but Lippos paid no heed. Hercules wasn't in pain; he just wanted this mind-numbing orgasm to continue as long as possible. On a whim, he licked sweat off of Lippos's nipples. The orgasms redoubled, causing Hercules to thrash about like a man having a grand mal seizure. Inside, he felt like a woman with a huge pussy for Lippos to fuck. A big muscle pussy. Just thinking about it, picturing himself being penetrated this way over and over again, Hercules went over the edge. He found his words.

"Oh shit, I'm gonna come." Even before the last words left his mouth, Hercules erupted a hot volcano of white come that leaped skyward before falling on his face and mouth. He licked it and groaned.

Lippos wasn't there yet. Hercules realized he wasn't either. That ejaculation was just a punctuation mark in the sentence of his intestinal quivering. That pleasure kept growing and building, doubling over and over, until, at last, his insides contracted in wave after wave of orgasmic convulsion. This time, the contractions were so powerful, they clamped down on Lippos's invading cock.

"Oh, Hercules, what is that? Why does it feel so good?"

Hercules was still convulsing, far beyond the reach of words to reply.

Lippos said, "Oh man. You're going to make me come."

If Hercules heard him, it wasn't clear. He was licking

his fingernails with a glassy-eyed stare. Another powerful wave of contractions hit him, causing Lippos to cross the finish line.

"Shit, man. Gods be damned! You're jacking me off with your guts! I'm going to—." He stopped there as a raging river of come shot out of him and smacked into the descending colon. Hercules needed more sweat. He licked and licked, each new drop sending him further into his orgasm. Lippos licked back; his ejaculation continued for several minutes. His balls were completely drained dry.

They remained locked together, cock in ass, lips on lips, tongue on tongue, and arms around each other. The contractions grew farther apart. The flood Lippos caused inside Hercules abated. In a swift motion, Lippos pulled out of Hercules. His cock was followed by a waterfall of come that puddled on the tiles. Hercules reached under, caught some of the effluence in his cupped palm, and drank it down. He caught a second handful by squeezing his own cock. He fed his come to Lippos. Then they kissed again, mingling the two loads of semen in their mouths.

Hercules finally regained his faculties. "You made me a woman today."

Lippos laughed and pinched a muscled teat. "You're the manliest guy I ever met."

Hercules smiled. "I know, I am. I'm the strongest man on Earth, but you still made me come like a woman."

"Is that what that was?"

Hercules nodded. "It was your sweat. It made me come deep inside."

The two men marveled at the effect each one's sweat had on the other. Lippos looked at the room, himself, Hercules. "We're filthy. How about a bath?"

❧ 15 ☙

A FAVOR

Lippos returned to the palace. No one had missed him. The king was not his real father, so why should he care about a bastard? Demetrius was on duty. He nodded at Lippos. Lippos returned the nod and said, "Tomorrow morning early."

Demetrius said, "I'm with you. Watch out for Basiliskos, though."

Lippos said, "He's still here? Shocking."

Demetrius stuck out his tongue and made an ugly face. They both laughed. Lippos climbed the stairs to his room. In the passageway, he ran into the King.

"Hello, Father. What brings you here?"

"I was looking for you. We need to talk."

Lippos felt his mouth run dry. He accompanied his father to the library, where they could converse privately.

"What is it?"

The King said, "I've had enough of pretending. You're not my son, and we both know it. I am married to your mother, but that is all."

Lippos bit his tongue to keep quiet.

"Furthermore, you're a deserter from the Athenian Navy. In short, you're a loser. I want you out of here tonight."

Lippos gasped. Basiliskos, the slimy, treacherous servant who caused this whole mess, appeared with a bundle. "Where shall I place it, my lord?"

The king waved him away. "Just leave it on the chair there. Lippos, those are your clothes and shoes. I'll let you have them. I even put 10 Obols in one of the shoes. You need to get out."

Lippos played what few cards he had. "My mother lives here, and you had my father killed. Where am I to go now?"

"You're a grown man. You can work for a merchant or a farmer. I don't care what you do."

Lippos needed to be in the palace for the plan to work. This was a terrible development. Basiliskos reappeared with a spear.

"Come on, horse dick, you're out." The ugly servant lowered the spear to a threatening angle.

Lippos grabbed the bundle and trudged downstairs. Basiliskos took great pleasure in prodding him with the spear.

Lippos whirled and grabbed the spear below the blade, catching Basiliskos off guard. He yanked it away and pointed it at the slimeball.

"I'm leaving. You don't need to escort me. Get back to your servant's quarters before I run you through!"

Basiliskos gasped and ran like a frightened child. Lippos threw the spear after him. It clattered to the floor. At the palace gate, he pulled Demetrius aside.

"Father threw me out. I need one more favor. You have to let me in tomorrow."

Demetrius nodded. "You can't come in the front, but I will leave the rear entrance ajar tomorrow morning when I start my shift."

Lippos fished out the bag with 10 Obols. "Here. I know it's not much, but I will reward you handsomely if your plan succeeds."

Demetrius looked sad. "I would trade all the treasure in the palace for your love."

Lippos whispered, "You have my love. You always will. I may be far away, but I will always love you, Demetrius. You were my only friend for many years."

Lippos didn't look back. He knew Demetrius was fighting back tears just as he was. He returned to the inn. The old lady didn't ask for money this time; she just shooed him back to Kallios's and Hercules's room.

When Lippos opened the door, Kallios lay atop Hercules, sliding his cock in and out. Hercules looked up with a guilty expression.

Lippos smiled. "I have good news and bad news. Bad news: I am no longer allowed in the palace. Good news: I'm not mad; I'm happy that you two are enjoying each other sexually. It makes me proud to have a lover who is so desirable. He's good, right?"

Kallios nodded.

"Then enjoy him. I'll go take a bath."

Lippos did feel a twinge of jealousy, but he appealed to his own better nature. They had both been inside Hercules at the same time. It's hardly fair to deprive his father. Lippos disrobed and stepped into the hot bath. He had so many thoughts swirling through his head. He wanted to kill Basiliskos, the disgusting servant whose gossip ruined so many lives. But if he grew philosophical, he supposed he could thank Basiliskos for indirectly putting Hercules in his life. If anyone should kill the wretch, it would be Kallios, whose life was utterly ruined by his serpent tongue. His mother would still be queen at Amyntor's side rather than languishing in a dungeon. Still, the truth is precious. Lippos learned who his real father was, and Amyntor ended the sham marriage that would have made her miserable, perhaps more miserable than she was now. It would all be better if their plans were to succeed tomorrow. When the groans from the room became audible, then ended, Lippos wrapped himself in a linen cloth and returned to find the two men sound asleep in each other's arms, their hair sticky from sweat and come.

Lippos slept on the floor.

❧ 16 ❧

ESCAPE

At dawn, the three men approached the castle from behind. Lippos tried the little-used door and found it ajar. Demetrius had kept his promise. Lippos held a finger to his lips. They tiptoed down the stairs until they were several floors below ground. Only torches offered light in this sunless place. Lippos led the way. They found the entire guard standing before his mother's cell. Demetrius gave him a key, and Lippos opened the cell.

On a plush bed of down and velvet, his mother lay sleeping. She was more beautiful than he remembered, though her skin was pale as chalk. He leaned down and put a hand on her shoulder. "Mother, it's me."

Phaedra sat bolt upright in fear. She looked at her son, and her face relaxed. "Lippos, my beautiful boy." Her eyes filled with tears as she hugged him close. "Basiliskos told me you were killed in a naval battle. How can you be here?"

That foul servant spread lies like oil on bread. "I shall have him killed."

"No, dear boy, he is my only lifeline to the outside world. He let me know how well you were doing in your classes. He brought me treats from the kitchen. He doesn't deserve death. He told me when they hung your father, too."

Kallios cleared his throat. "He doesn't mean ill, but he needs to get his facts straight and learn to keep quiet."

Phaedra's jaw dropped. "Kallios?"

He nodded. She ran to him and held him close. "What are you doing here? You're dead! We must all be dead for such a miracle to happen."

"The King spread a rumor that I was hung in the amphitheater, but he was kind enough to banish me to a deserted island in the Aegean."

"And who is this beautiful man?"

"Mother, I'd like you to meet Hercules." The big, muscled hunk shook her dainty hand. "He is my lover."

She beamed with joy. "I'm so glad you found love. I know what you had with Demetrius felt like love, but it was the kind that fades as youth is overcome with manhood."

Demetrius flinched. "You're right," he said, "I want a wife and children someday. I would have outgrown you, Lippos."

Lippos felt final pangs of regret when he said, "It is better that you find the love you need, not just the love you want in the moment."

The reunion was dragging on too long. Hercules said, "Where is the vault?"

Kallios helped gather the queen's vital belongings. She stepped out of the cell, and the guards stepped in. Kallios locked the cell door and left the keys just out of reach.

Several cells down was a copper door sealed with locks thicker than Hercules's forearm.

"Are you sure you can open it? We can go back."

Hercules laughed. "Watch this." He snapped the locks one by one and pried open the door. Inside was a king's fortune of gold, precious gems, pearls, purple dye, saffron, and a dozen other priceless treasures. The treasure was piled in coffers of various shapes and sizes. Hercules chose one that could be hidden under his lion's pelt. It was heavy with gold but felt light as a feather to him.

As the final step in their plan, Hercules slammed the door shut so hard, the palace quaked.

"Come on!" The three men and Phaedra climbed the steps rapidly. The only person there to stop them was the servant Basiliskos. He stood with arms on his waist.

"What, escaping, my queen?"

Hercules picked the servant up and threw him down the stairs. He turned to Phaedra, "Sorry, he was a big risk." They stepped outdoors, Phaedra holding her hand to protect her eyes from the sun. It was still early. They rushed into town and hopped aboard the sledge. Hercules placed the coffer in the cart and motioned for Phaedra to cover herself in blankets. Kallios sat at the front in one of Lippos's finest robes, looking every bit the nobleman. Lippos hid with his mother. Hercules pulled the sledge through town until they reached the road to Mount Lacmon. They passed out the gate as trumpets began to blast. No doubt, the king had raised the alarm. The portcullis slammed shut just as they were clear. Phaedra sat up beside her son.

"What plan was this?"

Lippos beamed. "Demetrius and the guards will tell of a monster, a hulk of a man, who came and stole you away, locking them in the cell. He also stole from the king's coffers."

"Did you dream that up?"

Kallios interjected. "It took three men to dream it up. Come, sit beside me, my love.

Hercules growled. "We need to get off the road for a while. I can hear horses and hounds."

He turned left where no road existed and plunged

them into a dark forest. He carried them across a stream and pulled them upstream in the same direction as the road. After a while, the sound of horses faded. They were probably ahead of them.

❦ 17 ❦

CAVE MEN

Hercules found a cave where they could all stay for the night. They were still in grave danger, but he sealed the entrance to the cave with giant boulders, adding significantly to their chances of survival. The cave was big enough to allow Hercules and Lippos to pair off in one chamber while Phaedra and Kallios got reacquainted in another. A small fire offered enough light to see by.

To drown out the ecstatic moans from next door, Hercules and Lippos got into a frenzy of their own. The change in Hercules was permanent: he would now always come like a woman inside his bowel but also ejaculate like a man. So when Lippos shoved his way in, Hercules let out a moan to rival Phaedra. Everywhere the humongous cock touched his insides, it sent a massive jolt of pleasure throughout his big muscular body. When the back-and-forth movement began, Hercules pounded the floor, rattling the nearby stones.

"Oh Lippos, you, you..." Hercules grew too ecstatic to speak. Lippos took another lick of sweat from Hercules and felt his biceps, triceps, quads, and hamstrings grow thicker. Hercules opened his eyes wide in surprise. "You're so muscular!"

Lippos grinned. "You have magic sweat."

"So do you, unhhhh!" A spasm passed through Hercules. He was already orgasming inside. The pleasure didn't sap his strength, only his ability to speak coherently.

"I wonder if I had another taste of sweat if this would become unbearable," Hercules thought. Not being one for slow decisions, he licked sweat from Lippos's chest. The intestinal orgasm didn't become unbearable; it just grew stronger. It caused Hercules to buck like a wild horse. It sent his cock stiffly skyward, lengthening it by two or three inches. He was not as big as Lippos or Kallios, but now he was in the same league.

Lippos guffawed. "Herc, you're huge! Did that come from me?"

Hercules nodded, awestruck by the size of his cock. At the same time, the waves of endless orgasm coursed all along the path carved by Lippos's impossibly huge, thick penis. Hercules focused entirely on his inner orgasm, saving his seed for planting in Lippos next. The orgasms grew ever more intense. Hercules thrashed about, cracking the stone floor with his fist.

"I'm coming! Oh gods, I'm coming!" Hercules cried out. Lippos sped up his fucking, thinking Hercules meant he was going to ejaculate, but that wasn't it. The rapid fucking made Hercules come over and over inside. The peristaltic waves stroked Lippos, causing him to grow that last bit thicker, plugging Hercules entirely.

"Hercules, your guts are jacking me off. I'm going to come." And with that, he spewed his semen deep inside the muscle man he loved with all his heart.

Hercules sat up, backing off of Lippos's cock. "Okay, my turn!" He couldn't wait to fill Lippos with his swollen cock that now hung to his knees.

Lippos wiped sweat from the brow of his lover and slurped it. He wasn't sure what effect it would have, but it had always been good.

Hercules licked the boy's butthole, being sure to use

plenty of spit. Lippos wriggled with joy. He had taken his father. It had been painful. Even Hercules, being so thick, was painful. And he hadn't let anyone inside him in quite a while. So he braced himself against the hurt. But when Hercules forced his expanded cock inside, no sharp pains came. Instead, there was a dull, pleasant ache. It was a type of pain that made anal sex feel good. None of the unpleasant twinges could break through. And the bliss that always kicks in shortly after the pain subsides was already there, and Hercules had only just entered him.

"What is it?" Hercules was worried by Lippos, whose eyes were wide open and unblinking.

"I think I know how it feels for you. I don't feel much pain at all. Don't stop."

Hercules pushed his way further, marveling at how much dick he still had exposed to the open air. He easily passed the colorectal junction, filling the sigmoid colon with thick, throbbing flesh. He kept pushing until his cock pressed against the descending colon.

What happened next was beyond anything Lippos could have imagined. Without the agony from anal sex to keep him in check, the pleasure was three or four times more intense than anything he had ever felt. And the touch of his lover so deep inside was enough to start the same kind of internal orgasm that Hercules had enjoyed. Lippos bucked and thrashed as wave after wave of contractions ravaged his guts.

"Oh shit, oh shit, oh shit, oh fuck." Lippos grabbed Hercules by the buttocks to pull him closer and deeper. There it was again, a brief but intense pressure on the descending colon. The new waves were out of sync with the first waves; they contracted in two different frequencies. Every so often, the waves would synchronize for a moment, sending Lippos into anal bliss so intense, he flew upwards, smacking his face against the broad chest of his lover.

Hercules was overjoyed by his new size. He loved the finality of reaching the end of the sigmoid colon and pressing that flesh button that made Lippos writhe and buck with pleasure. A couple of minutes earlier, he had been on his back with Lippos inside him. Remembering this was dangerous - he felt himself crossing the precipice. He tried to stop fucking long enough to get control of his orgasm, but Lippos's contractions were stroking his cock from stem to stern. He couldn't control it any longer. His balls tingled with imminent release.

"Lippos, I'm gonna come."

"Fill me up, Hercules."

And so he did. His muscular thighs quaked as his balls contracted over and over, pumping more and more come up the long shaft and out into the depths of the boy's guts.

"Don't stop."

To his surprise, Hercules stayed hard. He kept fucking Lippos, growing even thicker. He heard loud moans and knew he was doing it right. Lippos continued to stroke the enormous cock inside him with wave after wave of contractions. The mutual joy the two felt at that moment could only be expressed in a deep, loving kiss. Hercules's thrusts and Lippos's contractions were an orgasm machine. Hercules came a second time, then a third. Lippos never stopped coming. It was one endless climax from his rectum to his descending colon. When Hercules took his newly grown cock out of Lippos, the boy shivered, opened his hole, and ejected a cupful of semen onto the stone floor.

18

ON TOP OF THE WORLD

In the morning, Phaedra remarked on how Lippos had grown strong. Her son smiled and flexed his biceps, startling everyone, including himself. His arms were massive.

Kallios laughed. "Huge arms, huge legs, huge cock. You won the triathlon!"

They stayed in the cave for several more days until the search was called off. Every so often, they could hear barking dogs in the distant hills. With nothing to do, the two couples spent all their time in bed. Hercules and Lippos explored the limits of their newfound sexual prowess.

After three days, the barking ceased. Hercules, with the help of Lippos, pushed the boulders aside.

Hauling the sledge, Hercules never grew tired, but Lippos relieved him occasionally so the hulking beast could sleep. Lippos wasn't as strong as Hercules, but he still had no trouble pulling his parents and heavy Hercules through the forests and along the occasional trails that eventually led to the road to Lacmon Pass.

When the road grew too steep, Lippos could not help Hercules tow the sledge. This slowed their pace somewhat. They took frequent breaks, allowing Lippos to lay with his lover and improve on the pleasures they had discovered in the cave. The miles of mountain pass were pockmarked with the occasional puddles of come.

Even though it was late spring, the mountains were cold. Kallios and Phaedra wrapped themselves in blankets while Hercules enfolded Lippos in his lion pelt. He never felt safer.

"That's the pass." Kallios indicated a low point between Mount Lacmon and another smaller mountain. The sun dipped behind the hill. They set up camp far from the trail to avoid being passed by nosy travelers.

Hercules shared his lion pelt with Lippos. Their body heat quickly warmed them against the icy winds. They had been traveling hard; they were exhausted. Before either could muster an erection, they were fast asleep in each other's arms.

The following day, the goal was to cross the Pindus and find the source of the river Aous that flowed to Apollonia. By noon, they had reached the summit of the pass. It was the highest any of them had ever been. They were surrounded by clouds, which cleared and revealed much of Thessaly to the East and a good portion of Epirus to the West.

Lippos marveled at the sight. "What a magnificent thing is a mountain."

Phaedra put a hand on her son's shoulder. "Just a few days ago, I marveled at a beetle rolling a piece of dung across the floor of my cell. Today, I see the creations of the gods. Each act of nature is beautiful in its way, though I certainly prefer this view."

Kallios laughed. "That's sad and astounding at the same time. I never thought about nature in quite that way."

After they had lunch at the top of the world, Hercules easily towed Lippos and his family down the steep trail. By dusk, they had found the source of the Aous. Hercules set about converting the sledge into a large raft to hold all four of them. It grew dark, so they lit a campfire and settled down for the night.

Lippos wanted Hercules badly. He had never felt those internal shock waves before and wanted more. He positioned his buttocks at the tip of Hercules's newly expanded member and wriggled. The muscleman's cock responded rapidly, swelling and stretching. Hercules caressed the soft grey lips of the anus, marveling at how much it could look like a pussy. He spat in his hand and rubbed his cockhead until it shined. He spat again on the sloppy hole of his lover. Lippos couldn't wait. He grabbed Hercules by the dick and shoved it inside him. Instantly, his rectum responded with convulsive spasms of pleasure. Hercules pushed harder until he was deep inside Lippos. The boy thrashed and moaned, but he wasn't in any pain. No, it was pure ecstasy. He licked one more bead of sweat just to see what would happen. Nothing changed at first. Perhaps it would only work a few times, and then it would be over. Then he felt it. His buttocks were swelling with muscle.

"Lippos, your ass is huge! Oh, I love it!" Hercules spanked him hard. Lippos didn't even flinch. The changes inside him dulled all pain as the demigod's sweat worked its magic. His guts squeezed the muscle cock and stroked it. Each contraction gave pleasure to both men. As Hercules fucked his boyfriend's enormous ass, he thought more about the mutual pleasure. Just the mere idea of symbiotic sex caused his cock to swell inside Lippos.

"Oh, oh, oh Hercules! Oh shit! Harder! Fuck me harder!" Lippos was insatiable. Hercules pressed his pelvis against the huge ass cheeks and paused. He parted the cheeks and was able to go an extra inch deeper. He hit that spot that caused the convulsive waves to stroke up and down the length of his cock. He could have stayed still and would have come just from those intestines encircling and rubbing him. But he knew that Lippos wanted him to fuck hard. He unleashed the full power of his hips, no holds barred. Lippos was strong enough to handle him at full strength. He burrowed and backed out with violent thrusts. Lippos pounded the dirt, kicking up a tiny cloud of dust.

"Mmmnh yeah! Oh yes. Oh yes. Just like that, Hercules. Oh shit, I'm coming inside again!"

The waves were even more powerful in response to the battering ram that plundered the boy's intestines. Lippos saw stars before his eyes. It was too much pleasure. The last thing he remembered was Hercules plowing deep and then shooting his load.

Hercules stood over the immobile Lippos, who lost consciousness because he had too much of a good thing. After a few face slaps, Lippos came to.

"What happened?"

Hercules grinned. "I fucked you so hard you passed out."

Lippos got unsteadily to his legs. He knew Hercules had fucked him at full strength. He expected blood, pain, tender spots - but he was fine. In fact, he felt better than he ever had.

"My turn." Hercules lay on his back, his ankles raised skywards. Under his tunic, Lippos could see that hole, the first hole to ever take his cock in its entirety. The anus puckered and pushed out, opening a little, giving Lippos a little glimpse of paradise.

Lippos returned the favor. He fucked as hard as he could. It wasn't nearly what Hercules could muster, but it still had a strange effect on the muscleman. Hercules wriggled and twisted, trying to take more of his lover's cock inside. When the cock pushed past the sigmoid colon, it unleashed a wave of spasms.

Lippos, whose backside was tingling from the fucking he just got, had to gather his strength to fuck hard. He found his way and took very long, fast strokes that ended with another wave of contractions inside Hercules. The muscleman raised his head to see how much cock was going in and out of his hole. The sight of the thick flesh pumping in and out of him gave him a reverse orgasm that started at the anus and worked its way toward the intestines. The two waves met in the middle, causing Hercules to convulse so hard that he flew off the ground, taking Lippos with him. They landed in a tumble, rolling down the steep hillside until they landed in the icy river. It was shallow, and both men were insensitive to cold.

"Keep fucking me, Lippos."

"Are you sure?"

In answer, Hercules grabbed Lippos's firm, round buttocks and pulled him closer and deeper. Lippos continued his rapid fucking, enjoying the sight of Hercules thrashing in the water, scaring away all of the fish. Hercules found the icy water a huge turn-on. It contrasted so sharply with the friction heat inside his belly. He had another orgasm inside.

Lippos felt the contractions stroking his dick, and he came very close. He wanted to distract himself for a while to be able to give Hercules many more orgasms, but each one brought Lippos closer to coming. Then he saw the thick cock lying on the muscleman's chest. He bent down and put the tip in his mouth. He licked the piss slit and then shoved the head into his mouth. It was too much for both of them. Hercules had a dual orgasm, inside and in Lippos's mouth. Lippos swallowed the come hungrily. It excited him so much that he opened the floodgates and let a rushing river of semen fill Hercules's insides.

Lippos was looking more and more like Hercules. He would never be as big, but he was as big as a man his size could get. Hercules had a truly impressive cock, but it would never be as big as what Lippos was packing.

Other than those two differences, their bodies resembled each other in every way.

After washing off any stray semen or dirt from their bodies, they ascended the steep incline. Hercules smiled when Lippos hopped up for a piggy-back ride. He ran to the top of the hill, panting not from the exertion but from the excitement of his new longer cock banging between his knees.

19

CAPTURE AND RELEASE

When they awoke, Lippos saw horses surrounding him. His parents were bound in chains, no doubt under arrest. Lippos smacked Hercules to wake him. The blond demigod was groggy from sex and deep dreams. He blinked and took in the situation.

"Now come easily," said the lead guard. "We'd prefer not to run you through with our swords."

The king didn't believe the story about being locked in the dungeon by a lone muscleman. He would kill them if they failed at their mission. Demetrius was first in line for the chopping block.

"I've been so selfish. I never dreamed this would happen." All his dreams of Poseidonia went up in smoke. They were going to be executed.

Hercules leaned close to Lippos. "Hey, let's go back. Your father can't harm us."

Lippos was frightened, but Hercules gave him a re-assuring hug. "We'll be fine. These guys are your friends."

Lippos realized at that moment that he wasn't help-less in this situation. He had Hercules, but he also had the power of the throne. King Amyntor had never revoked his stepson's claim to the crown. He knew then what he had to do.

The speed of the horses shortened the long ride back to Larissa. Lippos rode with Demetrius so they could talk. Lippos shared his plans, and Demetrius agreed to play his part.

Instead of a week of walking, they were back in Larissa by nightfall the next day. The coffer was returned to the vault, which had since been repaired with new locks and a new door.

The four fugitives were each put in their own cell. Although Hercules could have broken them all out easily, he hid his strength from the King. He knew the long game Lippos was playing; breaking out was not called for until much later and even then, only as a contingency.

As agreed, in the light of early dawn, Demetrius came to see the prisoners.

"Can you get the king to come down to see us?"

Demetrius shook his head. "I don't know, Lippos. He's pretty pissed off. We need to let him cool down."

"It's best if he comes to us angry. Make up any excuse to get him down here."

A few minutes later, the King came storming down the stairs. He was followed by Basiliskos, who had walked on crutches since Hercules had tossed him down the stairs.

Lippos faced the king through the cell bars.

"Hello, father."

"Drop the pretense! Your real father is in the next cell over. We both know it. What do you want with me? To beg for mercy? Save your breath."

Lippos cleared his throat. "Well, Your Majesty, I wanted to negotiate your abdication."

"My what!? I'm building a scaffold for the four of you. You're in no position to negotiate anything! Abdication?"

Lippos persisted. "Yes, sir. I think we can come to agreeable terms."

Basiliskos hissed at Lippos. "You're insane. The King is going to kill you, and you are acting as though you have a claim to the throne."

Lippos smiled at the wretch. "I don't want the throne. I'm proposing an entirely new form of government. By the people and for the people."

The King sneered at his stepson. "Are you talking about democracy? Add that to the charges for which you will hang."

The King turned away, but Lippos stopped him. "If you were to die, I would assume the throne."

The King whirled around, "You and what army?"

As if on cue, the royal guards marched down the hallway in two groups that met in front of Lippos's cell. The King and Basiliskos were surrounded.

"You will all hang for this!" The king pointed an accusing finger at the men, who stood their ground.

Lippos flexed his muscles. "You can't hang your guards, your majesty. I've promised them each fifty gold coins if they support my bid for the throne. Who would protect you if you had no guards?"

Basiliskos pointed a finger at Lippos. "Traitor!"

Lippos smiled. "You told my secret and brought ruin on the family. Who do you think will be the traitor if I have the throne?"

The King waved his hand, "This is nonsense! Step aside." The guards would not part for the King.

Lippos said, "You haven't asked about my offer."

The guards lowered their spears, poised to run the King through.

"This is treason!"

Lippos smiled. "I loved you as a father growing up, and it broke my heart when you sent me to the Navy, knowing I would be killed in battle. But I never stopped loving you. That's why I want to make you a far better offer than death at the hands of your own guard."

The king stood his ground. "I'm not in a cage; you are. You're in no position to negotiate."

Hercules heard this and acted according to plan. He tore open his cell and approached the King.

"You can let him out willingly, or I can break him out. Which will it be?"

The King turned white. Such a show of strength brought home the hopelessness of his situation. "What are your terms?"

Lippos had no intention of being cruel. "If you could live anywhere in the world, where would it be? Other than Larissa, of course."

The King finally said, "I should like to live in Byzantium, on the straits of Bosporus. I traveled there as a child. It is surely the most beautiful city in Magna Graecia."

Lippos smiled. "You shall live out your days in that city. You'll have one coffer of gold to ensure your comfort. Basiliskos will accompany you as your servant. You may have two royal guards for your escort. Those are my terms."

The King smiled. "I taught you politics well." He turned to the guards. "Release the prisoners. I'm going to Byzantium. Lippos will give orders from this point on."

20

DEMOCRACY

Lippos organized the first election. He had no desire to rule. Heavy is the head that wears the crown. He nominated Demetrius for Archon, and he was elected. Representatives from Palasgiotis and other cities in Thessaly were elected. They came to the newly converted palace, which now served as the house of representatives and the home of the leader, Demetrius. The city prospered under the new form of government. Many improvements to trade and economics paved the way for a Renaissance.

Kallios and Phaedra built a modest home outside the walls of the city. Travelers often remarked how they could hear strange sounds coming from the house. It was just the sound of ecstasy that Phaedra cried when Kallios filled her ass with his long, thick dick.

Hercules and Lippos were not ready to settle down. They still longed to see Poseidonia on the Italian peninsula. Once the new government proved stable, they packed their belongings and prepared to retrace their steps to Apollonia.

Before they left, Demetrius called them into his chambers. Power suited him well. He was a just ruler and a dear friend.

"Lippos, I've lost you twice already. This is your

third journey away from Larissa, and I suspect you may never visit us again. I have a favor to ask."

He turned to Hercules, "May I fuck Lippos? You don't have to watch."

Hercules grinned, showing two rows of brilliant white teeth. "Only if I can join in." He stripped off his tunic, exposing his massive cock to Demetrius for the first time.

"Holy shit! You're nearly as big as Lippos!"

Hercules said, "A tad thicker, but nowhere near as long."

Lippos stood on the bed and sat down on Hercules's fat cock, letting the whole length snake its way through him. He lay on Hercules's chest, raising his legs to put them on Demetrius's shoulders. When Demetrius added his fat cock to the mix, Lippos felt a dull ache that he used to consider pain but now knew only as satisfaction. Demetrius oscillated back and forth while Hercules humped from below. Having both men inside him made Lippos happy. When they established a rhythm, Hercules in, Lippos out, then the reverse, it set off the contractions that Lippos craved every waking minute.

"Whoa, how are you doing that Lippos? You're jacking me off with your ass." Demetrius was astounded.

"Shut up and fuck me." Demetrius redoubled his efforts, causing paroxysms of pleasure in Lippos. Hercules got off on the way Demetrius's cock held so tightly against his, encased in spasming flesh. He sped up to match Demetrius, sending more contractions through Lippos's guts.

The orgasm was so intense that Lippos called a time-out. He needed to savor it alone. When the two men pulled out, it left a gaping hole lined with those grey lips Hercules loved so much. He wiggled the butt lips and spanked Lippos, whose hole clamped shut in response. Hercules tossed Lippos onto his back, his head dangling off the bed in front of Demetrius.

Demetrius asked, "Can I?"

Lippos opened his mouth wide in response. As the former guard pushed past Lippos's tonsils, Hercules forced his way into the sigmoid colon. Demetrius had never met a man or woman who could blow him, and he was so happy. With the semi-magical powers imbued in Hercules's sweat, Lippos could control his gag reflex and hold his breath for many minutes. Demetrius crept further and further down his throat with each thrust. To his astonishment, he felt the waves of contractions in the esophagus.

Lippos had his mouth full, so he could only moan through his nose. He had his first throat orgasm with Demetrius deep in his gullet. At the same time, he was having the more familiar contractions as Hercules tapped on the descending colon with the tip of his cock. The head-to-toe orgasm made Lippos swoon. He lost consciousness in brief intervals. Each time he re-vived, he felt the same orgasm building in his throat and colon. It would grow more and more intense, and then he would pass out again.

Demetrius withdrew his cock long enough for Lippos to take a few gulps of air, then he went right back in. The leader loved how long he could stay deep in his throat. It was the best blow job he ever experi-enced. No clumsy hands milking the shaft while licking the head; this was full-throttle oral sex.

Hercules fucked Lippos, holding his legs aloft and apart so he could see everything. He was so turned on by the sight of his fat cock disappearing into that mag-nificent hole. The peristaltic waves stroked the colossal beast, bringing him closer to orgasm. He yearned to feel Lippos inside him so he, too, could have that internal orgasm. But right now, he was focused on achieving a traditional orgasm and ejaculation. He was very close.

Demetrius couldn't hold it any longer. The throat stroking was so intense it pushed him over the precipice.

"Oh, Lippos, I'm gonna...' He fired loads of come down his throat. As he withdrew, he was still ejaculating, giving Lippos a taste of his manly come. Demetrius finished by coating Lippos's beautiful face in thick gobs of come.

Hercules saw the well-hung guard shooting come on his lover's mouth, nose, and eyes. The sight of so much come spraying out of the big tool put Hercules over the edge. With each thrust inward, he tapped the button that set off the contractions. He was pounding hard, barely holding back, as he felt the intestines cease their spasms because Lippos passed out. But then the boy awoke again, and the contractions began anew.

"Oh, Lippos, Lippos, I love you so fucking much!" Hercules bent to kiss him, getting Demetrius's come in his mouth. The taste of the come was the straw that broke the camel's back. "I'm coming!"

The demigod filled his lover with his come before collapsing on top of him, covered in sweat. He shook his hair like a wet dog to get the sweat out. A few droplets landed in Demetrius's mouth.

"What the fuck?" He felt his deltoids and biceps swell, followed by his triceps and quads. He was muscular when before he had been merely well-toned.

Hercules looked up and saw the changes. "Oh yeah, I should have warned you about that. Sorry."

Demetrius laughed. "I'm overjoyed. I only wish I could do that to my cock so I could be like you two."

Lippos said, "Funny you should mention it..."

Demetrius gained three inches after licking the sweat off of Lippos.

"Damn, I want to fuck again. I'm huge!"

Hercules offered up his ass. Lippos joined in. The muscleman had orgasm after orgasm on the inside, feeling the two powerful cocks stretch him like a sausage casing. Demetrius was a heavy comer. Mingled with Lippos, who was coming for the first time that night, it was a record-breaking lava flow of semen. It took Hercules ten minutes to expel the last of the jism from his bowels. The puddle that formed was the biggest yet. Hercules let out a powerful fart, and the last droplets landed in the pool of come.

21

SAILING AWAY

Demetrius waved a muscular arm to see the two lovers off on their journey to Poseidonia. Unlike last time, they had horses, two coffers of gold, and good food in the carriage. They rode quickly. Lippos enjoyed the feel of the horse's back on his stretched-out ass. It made him hard, which made riding difficult. He got his cock to stay on one side of the horse. His legs kept brushing up against it, adding to the problem. Then he realized it wasn't a problem at all. He gave in to pleasure, pinning the cock to the side of the horse with his leg. He rubbed back and forth for twenty minutes.

"Ohh. Oh shit!" He spurted come on the grassy trail beneath him.

Hercules turned and asked, "What's wrong?"

Lippos felt foolish. "I just came."

Hercules laughed. "It took you that long? I came in the first five minutes. I don't know how I will make this journey with these horses.

The two men left a trail of semen the whole way. Finally, they were spent and could come no more. They made camp near the base of the mountain. Sex was off the table for the evening because their balls were drained dry. But they wanted to be intimate, so Lippos devised an activity that he called "muscle worship". Each man would admire the muscles of the other, licking them, chewing on the nipple, massaging the back muscles, and playing with the butt until they were satisfied. It was incredibly arousing, knowing that it wasn't leading to sex but was a sexual act all of its own. Hercules flexed a bicep so big that Lippos couldn't get two hands around it. When Lippos flexed, Hercules nearly encircled the bicep with one massive hand. The play continued for hours until, finally, they were too sleepy. They fell asleep in each other's arms, their pinched nipples throbbing.

The next day, they reached the mountain pass and bypassed the campsite from their previous journey. By nightfall, they were on a trail in the foothills leading out of the mountain pass. They camped by the river and had intense muscle worship followed by anal sex. In the morning, they bathed in the cold river. A traveler passing by saw their enormous cocks and gasped.

"Oh, you poor things! So big. I'm sorry, I just couldn't avoid seeing them. They are rather large."

The traveler was an old man in a wagon.

Hercules wagged his cock at him. "You can do a lot more with a big one."

The old man smiled. "Don't I know it!" He lifted his tunic and revealed a massive cock.

"I never married. No woman would have me."

Lippos asked, "What about men?"

The old man nodded. "Yep. Plenty of them. But never found me a love like the two of you got."

As the traveler started his wagon again, Lippos felt sad. Why was he so lucky to have found a demigod that wanted him, and that old man had no luck at all? He pulled Hercules close and kissed him. They embraced, their naked cocks pressing against each other in the icy waters. Even cold, they were huge.

After a few more days, they at last reached Apollonia. They bartered passage to Poseidonia by trading their horses. The man with the boat got the better part of the deal, to be sure, but they couldn't take the horses with them, so it was fine. The two coffers that Hercules held were enough to buy every horse in Greece.

They set sail in fair weather. The ship's captain was young, barrel-chested, with meaty arms. He wore a tight tunic that showed off his bulbous ass. The two lovers couldn't help but stare. The sailor knew it. He wiggled his bottom for them, giving them both a hard-on.

The sailor dropped anchor.

"What's up? Why are we stopping?"

"Red skies at night, sailor's delight." He pointed to the setting sun. "I'll bet you can offer me some pretty big delights." To bring home the point, he slowly stripped off his tunic. He had a perfect penis, tiny, delicate, what nearly every man and woman wanted.

When Hercules undressed, the sailor gasped at the man's cock. "Oh, that might give more pain than delight."

Lippos unveiled his monster that dwarfed Hercules, and the sailor swooned. "No. No way."

It was a familiar refrain for both of them.

Lippos said, "Just the tip? That ass is so pretty."

The sailor blushed. "Yeah, a lot of guys tell me that. Oh, and women, too."

There were dozens of amphorae filled with olive oil. They had more lubricant in the boat than anyone could need.

"We'll be gentle, I promise." Hercules stroked himself to keep his hard-on. Then he caught sight of the grey ass-lips on the sailor. He was a well-worn hole, to be sure. "Something tells me, though, that you've had some pretty big things up your ass."

The sailor nodded. "Guilty as charged. I regularly get together with a fellow, and he puts his arm in there."

Hercules flexed, then grabbed his cock. "See that arm? My cock is much smaller than an arm."

The sailor laughed. "I was just playing coy. I saw your cocks swinging back on land, and I couldn't wait to get them inside me."

Hercules dipped his hand in the amphora and coated his cock with olive oil, then used two thick fingers to lubricate the entrance to the sailor's hole.

He pressed against the loose hole and found his way inside easily. He pushed past the rectum, then into the colon. The sailor sighed with pleasure. Lippos gathered a little of his sweat. "Here, try this." He opened his palm, and the muscled sailor took a lick. Oh! He was horrified to feel his cock growing between his legs. It was no longer a tiny penis. But it felt so good to have more down there. At the same time, Hercules bumped into the descending colon.

The sailor spasmed over and over. "What's happening? Why does this feel so fucking good?"

Lippos smiled. The sailor was shocked to see his cock rise and grow until it was four or five throbbing inches.

Hercules was gentle as he promised, but he didn't refrain from pressing the button at the end of the sigmoid colon that caused the sailor to spasm, stroking the giant cock with his guts. The sailor lay back on Hercules's chest and lifted his ankles skyward.

"You too, I can take it."

Lippos fumbled with the olive oil until his cock was slick. He pressed right where Hercules was already stretching the hole open and stretched it even farther. The sailor screamed.

"Should I stop?" Lippos was worried.

"No! No! Keep going."

Lippos slid his way into the man, his cock tingling as it rubbed against Hercules. He felt the spasms inside the flesh prison. He pushed past Hercules and hit the descending colon with two or three inches to spare.

"Go all the way. I'm used to it!" But he wasn't used to the orgasms that Lippos had introduced him to. As Lippos turned yet another corner and burrowed up the short man's descending colon, it caused shockwaves as strong as an earthquake inside. Hercules had never felt such powerful spasms. It was too much.

"Oh shit, I'm gonna come." Lippos felt the hot fluid surround his cock as Hercules dumped his load inside the little man. It was hard to resist the stroking convulsions. That and the warm sticky come making the chute slick was all he needed.

"Me too." He splattered up the descending colon. His thick cock blocked the sperm from dripping down until he pulled out, dragging Hercules with him.

The sailor was still convulsing. It almost looked like a seizure, but there was such a broad smile on his face they knew it was pleasure.

The sailor's new, larger cock reared up and shot copious amounts of come in the air.

"Oh, it feels so much better when it's big! How long will it last?"

Lippos shrugged. "I think it's permanent."

The sailor furrowed his brow. "I might scare away some men now. They'll think I want to fuck them. I never could before."

"Try it, you'll like it," Hercules said, bending over. He let the sailor fuck his ass with the modest cock until he had a second orgasm inside the muscleman's rectum.

"I didn't know what I had been missing. Thank you."

They lifted anchor at dawn and sailed past Apulia and into the straits of Messina. The island of Sicily, with its dramatic volcano Mount Etna, was stunning. The rains had turned the island the color of emeralds.

Another anchor, another night of passionate three-way sex, and they were off. They passed the islands of greater Sicily that were made of volcanic rock, and then they saw, on the shoreline, the magnificent temple of Poseidon towering over the city that bore his name.

THE END

THE GOSPEL OF
PRIAPUS

"Pedicare volo, tu vis decerpere poma; quod peto, si dederis, quod petis, accipies."

"I want to fuck some ass, and you want to steal some apples; if you give me what I want, you can take what you want."

— ANONYMOUS FROM *THE PRIAPEIA*

GOSPEL OF PRIAPUS
BOOK ONE

*Being the account of Contus Pedalis and his erotic friendship
with Chrysion Bipenna, whose sacred union strengthened and
healed all who partook.*

CHAPTER 1

In Lampsacus, Hellespont, in the period of
Augustus, a son was born to a family of modest
means. The son was Contus Pedalis, and like the
meaning of his name, he was well-endowed. The mid-
wife mistook Contus's magnificent member as a con-
joined twin.

As is common with extraordinary birth gifts, Contus's life was defined by his endowment. Word of the
peculiar birth spread throughout the Hellespont and
beyond. In the second week after Contus was born,
three holy visitors from Anatolia arrived to see the
babe. Upon seeing the peculiarly large organ, they
bowed in obeisance to the infant. They told his parents
that he was not an ordinary child but a demigod, born
of Dionysius, who must have visited and impregnated
the mother in secret. The parents of Contus agreed to
let the three holy men take him to their distant temple
in exchange for a small bag of gold. The mother wept

but knew that her child was destined for extraordinary adventures.

So it was that Contus and his wet nurse were carried away by boat and Roman Road to Istambolia. He grew up in a temple, far from the public eye. He was raised to believe that he was divine and that the gift between his legs was his source of power. When puberty struck, his hair became black as night, and a forest sprouted at the root of his cock. He grew taller, but so did his penis lengthen so that it remained at his ankles. Its thickness doubled until it was nearly as thick as his powerful thighs, grown muscular from carrying the heavy meat.

The many holy men inhabiting the temple were swayed by the cock's power. They felt a weakness or faintness upon seeing the magnificent member. Contus grew accustomed to attention and learned to draw power from the male gaze. When he bathed, it was a holy ceremony. The men formed a circle around him and manually brought themselves to orgasm, emboldened by the mere sight of his soft penis.

One day in his eighteenth year, a dove landed on the windowsill with a Roman gold coin in its beak. It was the first time Contus had seen money.

The dove sang:

> *Shut away for none to see*
> *You reek of young virginity*
> *You hide your proud divinity*
> *The world deserves it, doesn't she?*

Contus replied, "But fair dove, I stay in this temple for my safety. I don't belong in the world. What is this strange shiny stone you bring me?"

The dove sang in reply:

> *The coin is your inheritance*
> *From parents who sold you away*

> *To holy men who profit thence*
> *And put you on display!*

Contus reeled at the news. He had only ever known the temple. The brothers told him that he had no parents, for he was born of a god. This convenient lie kept the boy prisoner all these eighteen years. To hear of a family, worse yet, a family who sold him, was painful to his ears. He said, "Fair dove, I know not the purpose of this stone. Nor what you intend I should do."

The dove sang:

> *Take the coin to travel west*
> *'Twill pay for inns to take your rest.*
> *Find Chrysion, whom fate decreed*
> *Companion for your noble quest.*

Contus said, "I know not what lies West and have not heard of an inn. Nor do I know what my quest shall be."

THE DOVE FLEW TO THE HIGHEST WINDOW AND SANG one last verse:

> *Your quest will spread your fame abroad*
> *And strengthen the divine within thee,*
> *The gods have blessed your massive rod.*
> *I will appear whene'er you need me.*

And with that, the dove flew away. The holy men of the temple came for Contus as it was bath time. He tucked the coin beneath his pillow. In the sacred bath, he stood knee-deep and washed himself as the brothers gathered the energy from his phallus with their eyes. The excitement of the quest caused a stirring in his loins that he had never felt before. He grew lightheaded as blood engorged his member. The congregation gasped as the already enormous member swelled and reached upwards. Contus himself drew his breath in astonishment at the sight of his penis swelling, lengthening, and stretching skyward. He stumbled in his bath, dropping the sponge and sitting down hard on the stone coping.

All at once, a warmth rushed through him. His mighty testicles ascended. At the place where his member joined his body, he felt a vibration as a liquid moved through the ducts. He felt faint as his member throbbed and swayed of its own accord, then released a white river that cascaded into the bath for several minutes. The surface of the bath water grew murky from the semen that issued forth from Contus. He grew fainter still; then, all was dark.

He awoke in his bed. It was evening vespers, and he could hear the brotherhood arguing fervently over the meaning of the afternoon's events.

The eldest holy man said, "He has defiled the temple with his obscene display."

Another said, "It is a miracle. Contus touched not himself and gave forth issue of a hundred men."

Yet another holy man said, "It was not known to us that it could become aroused. The prophecy said that when such a sign appeared, we should cast him from the temple."

The eldest said, "Yes, but we have nothing written in our prophecy of the ejaculation. We cannot know for certain what should be done. Perhaps we must sacrifice him to the gods."

Contus Pedalis listened to the discourse. Upon hearing of the sacrifice, he gathered his pillow, robe, and gold coin and crept outside. He dressed himself to cover the gift and climbed a peach tree by the wall. He landed on the other side and made his way into the busy port town of Istambolia.

It was still light out, for it was the summer of his eighteenth year. He heard the sound of many people speaking and a kind of music that was new to his ears. He followed this sound until he entered the bazaar. Never in his life had he seen so many people in one place. In one row, merchants displayed bright spices on cloth-covered tables. In another row, there were musical instruments. A third row had tools and locks on display.

As he walked, he saw dozens of women. He had only ever seen girls delivering goods to the men of the temple, and he wasn't allowed to gaze at them. Now seeing women of all ages with their large breasts, he grew curious. They, in turn, were curious as to what was causing his robe to billow between his legs.

One woman put out a hand to stop him. She whispered in his ear. "I can offer my cunt at a very nice price."

Not knowing what a cunt was, Contus shook his head. "I'm looking for Chrysion."

"Who?"

"I was told to find Chrysion."

The woman waved an impatient hand in the air. "There are no whores by that name here, nor are there catamites. Chrysion is a male name. Try the market by the river. There are boys for sale there."

The dove told him the coin was for an inn, not to buy a boy.

"I'm looking for an inn."

A man overheard and took him by the arm. "I am Sylvanus. My family and I run an inn. I'll make you an excellent price."

The man named Sylvanus escorted Contus through the streets of Istambolia until he arrived near the waterfront at a large house with many rooms.

When Sylvanus demanded payment, Contus presented the gold coin.

"Son, that will pay for several years at this inn! I can't take your money. But I could not but notice on our walk here that you are blessed beyond all belief. If I may but see what springs from your loins, I will grant you a week's stay."

So Contus lifted his robe. Sylvanus grew weak and sat down hard. He stayed seated, searching for air, for several minutes. When at last, his breath returned, he stood. "Come, let me show you your room."

CHAPTER 2

The following day, after a generous morning meal, Sylvanus gave Contus directions to the boy market on the Bosphorus. Contus followed the water until he reached a large bazaar much like the one from the previous night. But this was different. There were no women or spices at this market. There were tools, leather garments, swords, and weapons, and many adolescent boys in various states of undress. Catamites.

A tall, virile boy approached him. "Two Lira for a visit to paradise."

Contus asked, "Are you Chrysion?"

The boy spat. "No, I'm Abel. Chrysion? What do you want with that piece of trash?"

Contus smiled. "You know Chrysion?"

The genuine innocence of Contus disarmed the boy. His scowl changed to a smile. "I know him. Hey Chrysion!"

From the long row of boys emerged a gentle, fair-haired youth. He opened his arms and came towards them.

"Are you Contus? The dove told me you would come!" His eyes strayed below Contus's belt. "Yes, you must be he, for I was told of your enormous blessing."

Abel looked down and whistled. "Gods, you're enormous! You could make much money with that!"

Chrysion took Contus by the hand. "We are to return to your inn, where I will lay with you."

Abel laughed. "He shall surely kill you if you lay together."

Contus frowned. "I have no desire to kill Chrysion."

Abel shrugged. "You don't understand me. But no matter. I have work to do."

Chrysion held hands with Contus as they retraced his steps along the water. When they got to the inn, Sylvanus greeted them.

"If you wish to have a guest, I will need to touch it."

Contus agreed. Sylvanus got on the ground and put his hand on the end of the massive pole. He stood, feeling the length until he reached the spot where cock and testicles attached to his crotch. He perspired and panted but remained standing, holding the flesh as heavy as a bag of stones.

"Welcome to the Inn."

Upstairs, Contus removed his robe. Chrysion's face showed fear.

"What is it?"

"The dove said I should lay with you, but I am frightened because it is too much of a blessing."

Contus was a virgin, and he had no notion what could be wrong with lying down beside him. "It is big, but there's room for you on my bed."

Chrysion laughed. The dove said you were pure, and I see what he meant. I mean to lay with you.

Contus was still terribly confused. Chrysion removed his robes, revealing his secret. He had a very large posterior but almost nothing in front. Contus had never seen such a small penis. The holy men were of many sizes but none so tiny as Chrysion; seeing it aroused him.

Chrysion stood pressed against the wall as the massive cock swelled and stretched upwards. Feeling faint, Contus sat on the bed. He had only just discovered this strange ability to grow and stretch, and it was upon him again without any way to control it.

Chrysion knelt in worship before the great phallus. He wrapped his arms around it, hugging it to his bare chest. With his tongue, he traced long lines up the shaft. He had to stand to reach the head, which resembled a large, red apple. He put his mouth on it and licked the slit, already flowing with clear semen. His tiny penis throbbed against the giant.

Contus had never been touched this way. The act of worship was familiar to him but only as an object to be gazed upon from afar. This act was a more profound communion, a uniting of his soul to Chrysion's. To be embraced by such a beautiful boy with such a perfect, tiny penis was holy.

Chrysion grew aware of the sacredness of their act. He had lain with many men, but none like Contus. Holding the massive phallus in his arms, licking and kissing the head, gave his mind clarity of purpose. He would consume the holy seed when it came.

Contus's breath grew more rapid. The sensation in his loins grew more intense. He felt bolts of lightning where Chrysion's tiny penis connected with his. A roaring thunder followed the lightning in his testicles. His body shook. Chrysion stroked the shaft, pushing Contus over a precipice. He ejaculated.

Chrysion swallowed over and over again, barely able to keep up with the cups of ejaculate that flowed from Contus's loins. He refused to waste a drop. When it was over, he had eaten enough to feed him for a day and night.

And so the first ceremony of Phallic worship was born; it became the guiding light for both young men. But a deeper communion was required before they could begin the quest.

CHAPTER 3

The next day, the two companions returned to the market where they met. Chrysion had a pouch of lead coins, the common currency in Istambolia. He purchased an ointment made of butter, lavender, and herbs from Babylonia with one coin. When rubbed on the skin, it reduces sensation. Chrysion had used this when he lay with men whose members were very large. It might help him manage the colossal task ahead.

On the road back to the inn, three men with dark souls stopped them. One wielded a scimitar and demanded their money—the other two held daggers to their throats. Chrysion handed over his bag of lead coins, and Contus had to surrender his gold coin, his inheritance. The men were about to cut their throats when a horse-drawn carriage passed by. Fearing someone might spot them, the three thieves ran. Contus ran down many streets in pursuit of the men. They entered a tavern, and Contus followed them in.

The man with the scimitar spun around as if to run him through. Contus side-stepped the sword and grabbed the man by the throat. With his other hand, he wielded his cock and slammed it into the man's head, rendering him unconscious. The two men with knives came forward. When Contus swung his huge cock at one of them, he tried to stab it. But the blade broke, and the colossal cock hit him in the throat. The man fell to the ground gasping for air. The third man held the money out, and Contus took it. The man tried to stab his hand, but Contus swung his massive penis and hit the man in the stomach. He doubled over and collapsed.

When Contus left the tavern, he realized he was lost. He found the waterfront and walked in the direction that should lead him to the boy market. But he was turned around and grew even more lost. He sat on the river bank and wept. He had never been lost before, having lived his entire life in the temple. He was afraid he would never find his companion or the inn. He looked to the sky and cried, "I am lost."

The dove who had brought him the coin landed beside him.

The dove sang:

> *In woods or city be ye lost*
> *Find the sun at any cost*
> *Follow the shadow to the inn*
> *Where Chrysion awaits within.*
>
> *And though you wish to start your quest*
> *To find your fortune in the West*
> *Your pole must enter Chrysion first*
> *Though pain ye cause, he will not burst*

Then she flew away. Contus followed the flight of the bird as it crossed the sun. He covered his eyes against the blinding rays. There was a massive temple with a tower that reached for the sky. The structure cast long shadows across the tops of houses for several blocks. Contus followed the shadow, and just as the dove promised, there was the inn. Chrysion was up in the room waiting for him.

"Did you retrieve the gold?"

Contus nodded. "And the lead, too."

Chrysion said, "But you have no weapon."

The strapping youth laughed. "But I do, Chrysion. I have a club so strong it will knock a man senseless." He grabbed his member for emphasis. "It cannot be cut by knife or sword, for it is holy."

Chrysion said, "I doubt it not, for you grow hard as chestnut when aroused. You carry a heavy club between your legs."

"I saw the dove today," said Contus, "He sang that I must enter you. What does it mean? I see no doorway."

Chrysion bent forward and parted his buttocks, revealing a cavernous hole. "Many men have lain with me. The balm of Gilead shall ease your entry into my hole."

The sight of the wide, dark hole caused Contus to swell quickly. He lost his balance and sat on the bed. Chrysion pushed Contus by the shoulders until he lay flat, the tower of flesh reaching high above him. He applied the balm liberally to his hole until it was greased and numb. Standing on the tips of his toes, Chrysion guided the apple-sized head to the entry. He pressed down until his buttocks parted, allowing the very end to enter. There it lodged, unable to continue.

Contus said, "I have entered you!"

Chrysion shook his head. "Nay, 'tis but the tip."

"But it feels good."

Chrysion smiled. "It is not enough. Keep pressing, and you will know pleasure unlike any other." Determined, the fair youth lifted his legs until he sat upon the flesh as though it were a tavern stool. Of a sudden, his hole gave way, admitting the whole apple at once.

Contus widened his eyes. "Gods, what is this feeling? Your buttocks embrace me!"

The youth nodded. "And you shall feel the full embrace if you are patient and temperate. Spill not your seed yet." Putting his full weight, the youth filled the first chamber with Contus's mighty flesh. As he learned in his trade, he leaned to one side, allowing the meat hammer to invade the second chamber. With much pressing and twisting, he filled the second chamber to the end. His eyes flapped like the wings of a butterfly.

Contus frowned. "I'm hurting you."

Chrysion nodded. "But it is a sweet pain." The second chamber was filled. When the mighty cock came in contact with the third chamber, Chrysion felt a holy union. In waves, his insides danced across Contus's staff. The cock was halfway in now.

The waves of holy spasms left Contus breathless. "I am close to spilling my seed."

Chrysion shook his head. "There's more. Refrain. Think of something else."

Contus thought of the woman in the bazaar, which distracted him from the intense pleasure that threatened to push him over the precipice. Chrysion grabbed the remaining flesh and pulled it inside him. The third chamber filled rapidly, stretching the boy's insides. It was a much longer chamber than the other two, and it accommodated the entirety of Contus. He sat on his knees, letting his buttocks come to rest on Contus's lap. He rocked up and down, stroking the holy monster with his insides.

"Gods, Chrysion, I fear I will not last long."

The boy nodded. "If you cannot wait, I am ready."

Contus grabbed the boy, pulling him down hard. The youth's eyes grew wide.

Chrysion said, "Oh! Bliss. Sweet Bliss." His tiny penis throbbed before it flowed with his seed, basting the face of Contus.

The larger youth was astonished. He tasted the sweet seed and closed his eyes. At that moment, he reached the summit.

"It is coming. The moment is here!" He groaned with pleasure as his giant testicles released their seed. He poured buckets inside Chrysion. The warm fluid filled the tight chamber, and when it had nowhere to go, the walls stretched even further. All the while, the spasms squeezed and nursed Contus's tremendous cock.

"I'll burst!" Chrysion pounded his fist on his lover's chest.

But there was no stopping the river. The seed pushed through into the fourth chamber. Chrysion breathed a sigh of relief. "Oh, Contus, I believe I love you."

Contus heard the words but was in the throes of holy communion with his lover. The spasms grew more intense, milking his great udder until it released more seed. He trembled with pleasure.

Then the spasms grew painful. Even as Contus softened, he still stretched Chrysion wide. Chrysion's body struggled to expel the great beast and the tide of seed behind it. The boy rose on his knees, but the great colossus remained wedged between the second and third chambers. Carefully he rose until, at last, the apple popped into the second chamber, then the first, each time making the sound of hands clapping. With force, Chrysion pushed the apple from the first chamber, clamping tight to hold the seed inside.

"Where is my issue?"

"It remains inside me; I cannot keep it long. My bowels yearn to expel it."

"It should not go to waste." Contus took the wash basin from the bedside table and held it under his lover's clenched anus. With a sigh of relief, Chrysius opened his hole, filling the wash basin with the holy seed.

Contus said, "This is my body and my blood. We shall drink of it."

They took turns taking large gulps from the basin until it was all gone. It satisfied not just physical hunger but spiritual thirst as well. The longing for connection to the divine was fulfilled by drinking the sacred issue of Contus's loins. It was communion.

When Chrysion bent to retrieve his tunic, Contus marveled at the abyss between his buttocks. "I made that," he thought. Without a questioning thought further, he leaned forward and licked the rim of the gaping hole. There he found more seed and was nourished.

He followed a line of semen down one thigh. Where

yesterday had been only soft boy flesh, today there were sinews. The buttocks were slightly more firm, and he saw cords of muscle beneath the soft belly fat.

"Chrysion, you have grown muscle."

The boy felt his abdomen, and indeed it was hard beneath the layer of fat. "It can only be a miracle of the holy seed."

Contus had tasted of the seed this day. He wondered if he, too, should sprout muscle or if his own body was immune to the healing properties.

"Shall we head West?"

"I should like to stay in bed with you a fortnight, but tomorrow we can leave."

They did not need supper. Chrysion lay nestled in Contus's arms, and they fell asleep in that loving embrace that resembles two spoons.

Contus awoke in the night to feel Chrysion's hand on his cock. The youth lay on his side, guiding the soft beast to his hole. With ease, he engulfed the soft head. As he backed into the giant, it swelled of its own accord. It reached the third chamber but could not pass further until fully engorged. As it grew, it climbed into the third chamber of its own accord. In this position, Contus could swivel his hips, pushing and pulling the great meat through the entrails of Chrysion. With the motion, the fair youth began to tremor and quake inside.

"Oh gods, Contus. You have made a vessel of me!"

The demigod imagined an amphora of olive oil, which hastened the production of pre-ejaculate, causing Chrysion's insides to become lubricated. The pushing and pulling grew less of a chore and more of a delight. It had the same effect on Chrysion, whose eyes disappeared into his forehead as he emitted a loud moan.

Contus grew confident that he wouldn't destroy the boy. He increased the pace, making loud clapping sounds as he entered and exited the third chamber. He lengthened his strokes, creating a clapping twice as he exited and re-entered the second and third chambers. With each clap, Chrysion shuddered in ecstasy. Once in the shape of a large 'S,' his innards had become a letter 'C.' They were rearranged to suit the needs of the god cock. Contus was grateful that Chrysion had cleared a pathway for him to enter heaven.

The light-haired youth shook involuntarily as the mighty cock brought his body into orgasm. His tiny penis followed, scattering seed on the floor of the room.

Contus was not finished. He had learned to withhold his seed and prolong his pleasure. Each in-stroke embraced his member in warm flesh, and each out-stroke held it, begging it not to leave.

Chrysion did not soften. His small penis throbbed anew. It was not from touching himself that he ejaculated again, but this time he caught the semen in his hand and fed it to Contus.

The black-haired god devoured the semen, as sweet and satisfying as his own. The taste remained on his tongue, reminding him of the great feast he produced between his own legs. The tingling on his tongue sent him over the precipice. In long, brutal strokes, he finished his work inside Chrysion, releasing a banquet of semen deep in his gut.

Together they caught the feast in the wash basin and consumed it.

Chrysion said, "Tomorrow, I shall grow strong as Hercules."

Contus nodded. "And I shall have two breasts like dinner plates."

The fair-haired lover laughed. "Forsooth, we shall have a vessel to dine on your semen."

Contus said, "I shall serve you nightly. Bring a spoon."

Then the exhausted lovers made two spoons and slept.

CHAPTER 4

In the morning, Chrysion said, "Contus, I fear my vessel is closing. I need you to open it again."

It was true. The ease with which Contus had entered the night before was gone. He applied the salve liberally to the hole, which had returned to its former state. With his fingers, he spread the tight valve until it was pliable. Chrysion knelt on the bed, his posterior aimed at his lover.

Contus grew aroused at the sight of his supine companion, and as he swelled, he put the apple-sized head inside. With some force, he entered the second chamber. At the third chamber opening, he met with great resistance.

"Chrysion, can you spare me entrance?"

The boy shook his head. "It is your task to open the gates; I have no power over them."

Stretching his arms, Contus was able to grasp his waist. With force, he pulled the fair youth to him. The mighty god cock penetrated the third chamber and easily slid upwards to fill it.

Chrysion cried in pain. His insides were learning to accept the holy penis, but the change was painful.

Contus asked, "Are you hurt? Should I stop?"

Chrysion shook his head. "It is a good pain that turns to pleasure. Please continue."

Contus felt his pubic hairs brush against the boy's buttocks; he was all the way inside.

Holding Chrysion by the waist, he pulled back as far as his arms allowed, then pushed forward, holding the boy to keep him from falling off the edge of the bed.

"Ohh! Ow! Ohh!" Chrysion wavered between pleasure and pain.

Contus found a rhythm and kept it like the regular beat of a large drum at ceremonies. The double claps kept time as he plunged in and out of the inner chambers.

"Ohh! Yes! Yes!" The pain gave way to ecstatic bliss. Chrysion trembled and quaked inside.

Contus had cleared the path again so that his penetration required less effort. He leaned over his lover and held his shoulders, his powerful chest resting on the boy's muscular back. Instinctively, he kissed Chrysion's neck.

He whispered in his ear. "I should like to do this with you for all eternity."

The boy couldn't answer; he was too deep in blissful union. He made animal grunts instead. He held his torso aloft with both hands; he could neither touch himself nor his lover. But in the short time they were together, Contus had learned when Chrysion was about to ejaculate. It was a subtle quickening of the breath and a tightening of the anus. He put one giant hand down there and caught the seed, which they shared, sipping from his cupped hand.

The elixir again had the potent property of pushing Contus past the brink of orgasm. Holding Chrysion by the neck and hair, he drove his seed deep inside the boy. As was befitting the god of cock, Contus never had a small ejaculation, and every time it was enough to fill a wash basin.

Chrysion squatted over the large bowl and released the holy milk. Together, the god and the boy took turns feeding on the semen until it was gone. They were full and satisfied.

Chrysion said, "I know now you are a god, for my insides are healed of every wound by your seed."

Contus blushed. "I am a mortal. I was born of man."

The fair-haired boy said, "The gods can plant seeds in mortals and produce more gods."

The darker boy said, "If that's true, then have I planted a god in you?"

Chrysion burst into laughter. "Had I a womb, I fear you may have planted a god in me. But I am content to worship your god-given gift. You may plant all you wish, for I am the happier to accommodate such greatness."

CHAPTER 5

It was still early. The two lovers, one mortal and the other a god, left Istambolia on their mysterious quest. They took the road in the direction of the shadows, heading West towards Thrace.

They passed merchants, beggars, soldiers, and politicians on the great Roman road. Many gasped in astonishment, for they could see the outline of Contus's mighty cock through the fabric of his robe. But none stopped to speak. It was a well-worn, passable road connecting Asia Minor to the Northern Roman Empire. Their feet grew tired after many thousands of steps. They saw the lights of a small town on the horizon. There they would stay at an inn and continue their rites of the worship of cock.

The inn was small and humble. The owner asked for only one lead coin for a night's stay, which included wine, bread, and oil for dipping. Having eaten nothing all day, the two were grateful for the meal. The wine was strong; the two became drunk. They ascended to their room, tasting each other's mouths and lips. With haste, they removed their garments and began the worship of the phallus. Chrysion kissed the tip, licked it, rubbed it, and watched as it doubled in size, then tripled. Letting go of the massive beast, he bent to remove his sandals. As he stood, Contus swiveled and accidentally clubbed him. The boy fell unconscious.

Chrysion awoke in the morning with a terrible headache and a bump on his forehead. Contus wrung his hands worriedly, not noticing that Chrysion was awake.

The boy spoke. "You wield a powerful club, friend. It's your lightning bolt of Zeus or your spear of Pallas Athena."

Contus rushed to his side. "Are you well? I feared I may have killed you, for you wouldn't wake."

Chrysion smiled weakly. "I am fine, but my head aches."

"Mine too. The wine was not pure, I fear."

"We must worship, and in so doing, will gain the elixir to bolster our strength for the road."

And so the two nourished one another with their seed, and their heads ceased to ache.

"The communion of seed is good," said Chrysion, "for it gives us strength and heals our ailments. We must share the good news, for you are a great physician of the gods."

In the tavern downstairs, a large, swarthy man wept into his cup of wine.

Contus put a hand on his shoulder. "What brings you sorrow, brother?"

The man lifted his head, wiping tears from his red eyes. "I am a wrestler, but I suffered an injury yesterday and now am lame."

He pointed to his leg, which bore a splint. "I can no longer earn my keep."

Chrysion spoke. "Fortune has brought you to us. We have only just learned of our healing powers and seek to share them with the world. Care you for a cure?"

The wrestler frowned. "I can scarce afford the ointment or draft you are peddling."

"We give it freely, for it costs us nothing to make."

"Then there is naught to lose. How do you cure me?"

Contus said, "Come upstairs to our room, and we will heal you."

The wrestler pointed to his leg. "I can no longer climb stairs. I stay in the manger. Can you perform the miracle there?"

The two lovers nodded. Together they helped the powerful wrestler to his feet. With one arm around each boy, he hopped outside to the barn where he slept.

Chrysion whispered to Contus. "I doubt you should try to enter him. He appears to be an active lover, not a catamite."

Contus nodded. He said, "O Dove, how can I heal this man?"

The dove flew down from the rafters and sang:

> *Contus puts the cock of god*
> *In Chrysion, the physician*
> *The patient joins the mighty rod*
> *Thus mingling their emission*
>
> *Chrysion's seed shall stitch the flesh.*
> *And Contus mend the bone.*
> *But patient's seed shall seal the scroll*
> *Communion shall be known*
>
> *And when at last communion ends.*
> *The patient, too, can heal.*
> *For you have passed the gift to friends*
> *Through semen's sacred seal*

And the dove flew out of the barn into the bright morning sky.

With that explanation, the healing duo knew they must become a trio to heal the wrestler.

"I am Contus, and this is Chrysion. What is your name, sir?"

"I am Dyemuya, the legendary wrestler. Have you heard of me?"

Chrysion said, "Yes. I have seen that name on posters in Istambolia. You are famous."

The wrestler grinned. "I am. But have you not heard of me, Contus?"

Chrysion answered for him. "Only a few days ago, he had been cloistered in a temple his entire life. He had no opportunity to know of your greatness."

Dyemuya chuckled and grabbed his bulging crotch. "Greatness indeed."

The wrestler, overflowing with confidence, had only looked Contus in the eyes. Having spoken of his own penis, he did as all men do and looked at the others. Chrysion revealed nothing, of course, but when he saw the serpent between Contus's legs, he started. "Gods, but you're blessed!" His gaze continued downward. "Is that your cock I spy at your ankles?"

Contus nodded and smiled. "Fear not, though our cure requires seed, I will not enter your sacred pathway. Together you and I will fill Chrysion with our seed."

The wrestler looked doubtful. "How is that possible? You surpass a horse in girth and stature."

Chrysion spoke. "I am a vessel for his seed. As much as he is gifted in size, so too am I blessed internally with depth.

The talk had aroused the wrestler, whose prick reached skyward. By any mortal account, it was massive, but it was nothing compared to the god cock of Contus.

Dyemuya lay on his back on the soft hay, his legs open wide and his cock standing straight up into the sky, more than half a cubit in length. It was as big around as it was long. Chrysion sat upon it. As quickly as a baby takes a breath, he inhaled the giant cock until it came to rest in the second chamber.

The wrestler commented. "When I lay with catamites, I often hear them scream. You offered no resistance."

Contus stood between the wrestler's legs. "That's because he has grown accustomed to my holy member."

The wrestler had seen it through his robe, but he trembled now that it was exposed. "It's so powerful; I felt it in my heart. It's magnificent to behold."

Contus nodded. "You can draw power by gazing upon it, but this will heal you."

Carefully, Contus pressed the head of his cock to Chrysion's opening. As though the gods themselves willed it, he entered him with little force. The power of his cock rubbed off onto the wrestler's cock. Easily he passed out of the first chamber, past the end of Dyemuya's cock, and into the third chamber.

The wrestler was fascinated by the large round buttocks on Chrysion. He rubbed them as Contus did the hard work, sliding betwixt the walls and the wrestler's massive cock.

As he was wont to do, Chrysion began to spasm inside.

"Oh, Apollo and Aphrodite, what is that?" The wrestler's eyes opened wide. "I feel as though a hand were inside you, stroking me!"

Chrysion said, "That is the beginning of the healing process." Then his eyes looked skyward until they were inside his forehead, and he knew bliss.

Contus knew that the more ferociously he fucked, the stronger the medicine. With savagery, he impaled Chrysion repeatedly, building heat and friction against the wrestler's long, thick cock. All three men had passed into an ecstatic communion. There were no words, only animal sounds.

Chrysion's breath grew shallow, signaling the imminent release of his seed. Contus put the wrestler's meaty paw in the path of Chrysion's tiny penis so that he caught all the seed as it sprayed forth.

Silently, with great reverence, the wrestler sipped the precious fluid before passing it to Contus, then

Chrysion himself. He circulated it a second time until his hand was licked clean.

In the brief time it took for the trio to lap up the holy fluid, Chrysion again took many light breaths. This time the wrestler raised his hand unaided and caught the second helping of semen, which was even more than the first. As they sipped, Dyemuya reached the summit.

"I've arrived. Here it comes." All three men felt the hot blast of fluid that coated Contus's cock and lubricated Chrysion's insides.

Contus slowed his furious pounding, then held himself all the way inside his lover as his hot semen flooded the third chamber and leaked into the fourth. The barn was silent but for the heavy breaths of the three men. They stayed locked together for several minutes, enjoying the manly exchange of energy.

At last, Dyemuya softened and slipped out of the hole. Contus carefully withdrew so as not to spill his holy seed nor the wrestler's sacred semen. In a milk pail, Chrysion emptied his bowels of the precious fluids. The wrestler marveled at the enormous quantity of semen.

"Mine is but a fraction."

Contus nodded. "I think it's enough. Drink."

Dyemuya drank freely from the milk bucket. He wiped his lips with his wrist and passed it to Chrysion, who drank enough to satisfy. Contus drank much, too. The milk pail was still full. They passed around the bucket repeatedly, growing drunk on sperm. Dyemuya took the last swallow and burped.

"I'm so full; I may never eat again."

The three men lay in the hay, looking at the barn rafters.

The wrestler broke the silence. "How long does it take?"

Chrysion said, "You're our first patient, and we have

only tasted of the healing seed ourselves. But it worked fast when I was sore inside.

Dyemuya lifted his leg and moved it. "There is pain, but it is much less."

Contus said, "My seed is knitting your leg bone back together."

Chrysion said, "And where the bone has broken through the flesh, you will see the skin has healed."

Dyemuya drew up his tunic and found only a faint scar. He loosened the splint and removed it. His knee bent and straightened.

"This is a miracle. I must pay you!"

Contus shook his head. "It costs us nothing."

"But it's the work of the gods themselves. Surely you put a price on that!"

Contus stroked his chin. "Spread the good news. Tell them of the holy seed. Share your seed; for now, it is imbued with healing powers, too."

Dyemuya wept, but now it was for joy, not self-pity. "I have the healing power, too?"

Contus nodded. A little bird told me so.

CHAPTER 6

Dyemuya had a horse and cart. The lovers could heal the day's blisters with communion, but the wrestler was traveling west on the road anyway. They accepted his offer of a ride to Thrace.

"In Uskudama, I will wrestle in the competition, and I often win, despite not being as powerful as the other wrestlers. Do you know my secret?"

Chrysion shook his head.

"This." He pointed to his cock.

Contus said, "I don't understand."

Dyemuya grinned proudly. "I am much, much bigger than the other wrestlers down there. Many of them are hung like Chrysion...no offense."

"None taken"

Contus shrugged. "I still don't get it."

The wrestler gave a wink. "We wrestle without clothes. Not only does my superiority give me advantage over their mind, but there is also a rule that disqualifies anyone touching another wrestler's cock with their hand."

The three travelers laughed heartily.

Dyemuya said, "Hey, imagine if you wrestled, Contus? You're strong enough, and you wouldn't surpass thirty seconds before your opponent was out of the match."

Contus smiled. "I don't know that it would further my mission."

Chrysion interjected. "It would be a way of spreading the good news. By exposing your member to spectators, your fame would spread, and so too the knowledge of your healing. You could act as physician to the wrestlers."

Contus sat up straight. Chrysion was right. There were many athletes in need of his healing powers. But what if they were too small to share in communion? How would he heal them then?

THE DOVE LANDED ON THE EDGE OF THE CART AND sang:

> *The small shall gain your healing too*
> *They stand before your face*
> *You drink from them their tiny spew*
> *And thus impart your grace.*

And away flew the dove as quickly as she'd arrived.

The road to Uskudama was four days' travel by cart, so the three shared rooms at inns along the route. They avoided the wine, which was terrible in that region.

When Chrysion broke bread, his biceps bulged. A few days earlier, his arms were soft and weak.

Contus said, "My seed has made you strong, friend."

Chrysion grinned. "I have never felt such power."

Dyemuya, the wrestler, listened intently. "You say you had no muscles before?"

Chrysion shook his head. "I was a boy less than a week ago, and I'm now a man. My chest has sprouted thick hairs, and my beard is growing in.

The wrestler blushed and said, "I should like to partake of communion once again, that my leg grows stronger."

Contus agreed. In the room, when the three travelers had filled their basin and drank their fill, Chrysion flexed his muscles. He was no longer shaped like a pear but an inverted triangle atop two powerful legs. His penis did not grow. His power came from the tiny member. He was happy, for as a catamite, men revered his small penis as beautiful. He never wanted it to change.

Dyemuya, however, would gain power in wrestling with the growth of his member. His desire to grow bigger mingled with the communion seed. On the third night, when he checked, it had grown closer to his knee. He was nearly two-thirds of a cubit now in length and girth. He flexed an arm and stared in amazement at his massive bicep. His chest had grown more pronounced so that his nipples pointed downwards on the hillocks of his breast.

Late the following evening, they arrived in Uskudama. Dyemuya drove the cart to the wrestling arena. It was little more than a square patch of grass with many wooden seats on risers. Adjacent to the wrestling green was a large building housing the local wrestlers and any visitors. Dyemuya spoke with the owners of the building and secured two rooms.

"We can stay here for free, but there's a wrestler

who cannot move his legs, and he has paralysis. Can you share communion with him?"

Contus nodded. "Take me to him."

The injured wrestler, Koipides, sat in a chair with carriage wheels. He traveled by means of his arms.

Dyemuya asked, "Are you in pain, brother?"

Koipides said, "I feel no pain, which I fear is worse. I cannot move my legs. Perhaps a witch has hexed me."

Contus touched the legs made soft by immobility. He put a hand on the man's penis.

Koipides turned his head sharply. "I feel that, sir. What do you intend?"

It was not a large penis, nor was it small. But it was soft. Contus said, "I need to manipulate it to see if you can grow."

The man said, "Certainly, I can grow. Not like Dyemuya, but I am larger than many."

Contus determined that it would not pass into the second chamber and was, therefore, not suitable for the communion of twin penetration. He would have to try the second method.

"You will find my healing method pleasant but strange. If you doubt, know that Dyemuya was lame four days hitherto."

Koipides agreed to the peculiar ritual, despite feeling distaste for union with men. If it restored his withered legs, he would do anything.

The coordination to achieve this communion was made more difficult by Koipides's inability to stand with his cock at mouth level. Contus was perplexed, but Chrysion, having worked as a catamite for many years, was an expert in complex arrangements. He lay face down on the bed, and Contus lay perpendicular, forming a cross, entering from the side. His head rested in the patient's lap, allowing him to take communion directly from the penis.

Because the injury was so severe, Dyemuya offered

to give communion directly to Koipides. In this way, the healing energies would multiply.

The crippled man sucked seed from Dyemuya, drank Chrysion's sweet boy seed, and consumed large helpings of Contus's holy seed gathered from the anus of Chrysion. He was the last to give his seed, for his loins were much impaired. When the communion issued forth, his toes curled. Contus kissed each man, sharing the seed of the cripple with them. Koipides gave a gasp of surprise when his legs twitched.

"I feel my toes! I feel my legs!"

After several more days of these complicated communions, Koipides rose from his chair and walked. The news traveled quickly among the athletes. A holy man, a healer, walked among them.

CHAPTER 7

Contus trained with Dyemuya for the competition. First, they stripped off their clothing. Next, they doused each other in olive oil to make their bodies slick. With a judge on hand to oversee their trials, they wrestled. Over and over, Dyemuya was disqualified, as his hands couldn't avoid touching the colossal cock. As long as both men concentrated on areas above the waist, they remained in the match. But the match could never end with a navel pointed skyward without a move below the waist. Many matches lasted hours while the two men grappled, penises touching, causing arousal.

There was no rule against one man's penis in contact with the other, so they did it often, despite the ensuing erections. Once they were both erect, with cocks pointed skyward, they could reach below the waist. There were no rules against ears or faces touching penises, only hands. So they found they could only wrestle when fully erect. The judge was certain there should be a rule against wrestling in this condition, especially with two men so greatly endowed (for now, Dyemuya's penis was a full cubit in length and three-fourths in girth). But only a committee could rewrite the rule book, so the men entered the match as opponents.

On the day of the fight, Chrysion oiled up both men, taking extra care to rub oil into the deep folds of the two massive penises. He rubbed until both men were aroused and kept them in a constant state of arousal until the announcer called their match.

The spectators were astonished by the massive cocks. No matter that Contus dwarfed Dyemuya, they were both large enough to be seen in the highest riser. Wrestling entirely below the waist, if one man became soft, it would lie on the shoulder of the opponent, who would use his ear or forehead to stimulate the opponent back to full arousal. In this way, the far more experienced man won the match. Contus lay belly up, cock covering his face. The crowd roared.

Dyemuya wrestled until he reached the final match. In every fight, he could defeat his challenger by skill and by reason of his enormous cock. At the contest's climax, Dyemuya was the champion because the reigning champion touched his huge member and thereby lost the crown.

As the contest disbanded, well-wishers and the curious came to speak with the two men. Many touched the great god-phallus or stroked the lesser of the two.

Arslan, A local patrician, invited Dyemuya and Contus to his home in the hills above Uskudama. He promised figs from Africa, spices from the Indus, and meats from the forests of Dacia.

Dyemuya thought quickly. "Only if each can bring a guest."

The patrician waved his hand. "But of course. Bring who you like."

Dyemuya brought Koipides, who had regained his

strength and grew more robust than before the fall. Contus brought his fair-haired lover. The four were all healers now, for they had partaken in communion, and the sacred seed of Contus Pedalis coursed through their veins.

Arslan took no wife. He lived with Gyorgi, a boy lover who served him with great devotion. As promised, the table overflowed with delicacies from throughout the Roman Empire. As the men ate, a band played haunting melodies on horns, flutes, and drums. The music was as intoxicating as the wine from Etruria. The mirth and merriment gave way to confessions of lust.

Gyorgi said, "Dyemuya, I have longed for your cock inside me since I first attended a match many years ago. Now it is so big that my desire has multiplied a hundredfold."

Dyemuya stood and removed his tunic. "Come to me, boy, and take what you will."

Gyorgi disrobed, revealing a diminutive penis much like Chrysion's, but not as pretty and not as small. Dyemuya dropped to his knees and buried his nose in the boy's posterior, making it wet and slippery with saliva.

Arslan gestured to Koipides. The athlete came to the patrician's side, and they kissed. Koipides had grown in length and girth as a side effect of the communion. The patrician stroked it but surprised him by revealing a regal cock rivaling Koipides's in size and strength. A four-way union was formed, with Dyemuya inside Gyorgi, Arslan inside Koipides, and Gyorgi taking direct communion from the cock of Koipides.

Contus held Chrysion's hand. "We have formed the first church of the sacred seed. These men will not waste a drop; all will partake of the holy communion. The healer's gift will pass to these two new men, and the church will grow.

Chrysion said, "I wish to take private communion with you."

Contus emptied a fruit bowl, then brought his lover to the balcony overlooking Uskudama, Orestia, and the confluence of the Tonzos and Evros rivers. Chrysion stood at the railing and bent, so his gaping anus was accessible. Contus walked forward until the apple was against the peach. He met very little resistance as he stepped closer. Chrysion's entrails were accustomed to the invasion and welcomed him warmly. His moans were not cries of pain; they were howls of ecstasy. Every moment his lover was inside him was a glimpse of paradise on Earth. He was in the garden of delights, swallowing the apple whole. In just these few days, Contus had surpassed the skills of any client Chrysion had served. Because the gods created his phallus, it was only fitting that they should have blessed him with an extraordinary natural skill in the sexual arts. What better teacher than the highly skilled catamite, Chrysion?

With the fat layer gone, Chrysion's abdomen revealed the outline of Contus's cock on its path in and out of the third chamber. Chrysion put a hand on his belly and squeezed, pinching the giant cock between his fingers.

Contus shuddered at the new sensation. The fair-haired youth's insides began to spasm. The waves of peristalsis massaged his member and hugged it from the inside. As before, Chrysion's breath grew rapid and shallow. Contus put a hand below and caught the effluence. He fed it to his boy before lapping up the remaining sweet nectar.

They were so tuned to the signals of each other's bodies that they could anticipate each progression. Chrysion felt the enormous cock grow more slippery as the clear seed lubricated his passageway. He knew it would be soon that Contus climaxed. This knowledge aroused him, and his breath grew shallow once more. Again, he spilled his seed into his lover's hand, and they both partook.

Contus took shorter and shorter strokes, a sure sign that Chrysion's entrails would soon fill. "I'm here." He flooded the boy with his sacred communion, the body, and the blood. He held Chrysion's head close to his and kissed him while the endless flow of semen continued. Each time they did it alone, the flow was more. They had produced too much. Chrysion squatted and filled the fruit bowl almost to the top. They took large gulps, but they wouldn't finish. They brought it to the orgy in the dining room and fed it to the four men and the three musicians.

Arslan stretched out his hand. "I have suffered from arthritis for ten years, and now I can stretch my hand. What is this miracle?"

Chrysion and Contus explained the miracle of the holy seminal communion. Arslan listened closely.

"I shall build a church right here in Uskudama and consecrate it to the healing of physical ailments."

And so the first Temple of Phallic Worship was born.

GOSPEL OF PRIAPUS
BOOK TWO

Being the account of the travels of Chrysion Bipenna and Contus Pedalis to the Macedonian city of Thessaloniki, where they meet Kolossos, discover the fertility embodied in the seed of Contus, and the Temple of Praiapus receives its name.

CHAPTER 1

After seven seasons of wrestling, the dove appeared again to Contus and Chrysion. It sang:

> *A single church shall grow in time*
> *But time is up; the clock will chime*
> *Faster will the church be spread*
> *If you but travel where you're led.*

With much sadness, the duo announced to the church, which had grown to thirty members, that they must depart to form new churches abroad. The athlete Dyemuya, whose member had swollen to an impressive size exceeding a cubit, was ordained as the church's first minister, so Contus was free to depart. Many boyish men with tiny penises like Chrysion's could fulfill the role, but Gyorgi was appointed high priest because he was the first to give sweet seed without Chrysion present.

Arslan provided them with a heavy bag of silver and a horse and cart with wheels calibrated for the Roman Road to Athina. The wheels fit perfectly in the ruts.

CHAPTER 2

On a warm day in Autumn, they departed, taking the southwest road in the direction of Macedonia and Achaia. The distance was nearly 600 miles. They could cover 80 miles in a day or 100 if they started early and finished late. But they found the horse couldn't go more than 75 miles a day, so they were obliged to stay in several different inns in towns and cities along the Macedonian coast. The road was not always smooth. A wheel came off the wagon outside the metropolis of Thessaloniki. The two men gathered their most essential belongings and abandoned the cart. Although they had no saddle, they could fashion saddlebags out of large blankets and rope. Chrysion rode the horse until Contus grew tired, then they switched.

After the ten-mile journey into town, they realized they were overdue for a bath. The inn they chose had no bathing facility. The innkeeper advised they go to the thermae, a traditional bath. When they arrived, the attendant showed them to the changing room. After removing their vestments, a boy took their belongings and placed them in a locked chest, giving the key to Chrysion. The boy stole nervous glances at Contus's magnificent appendage, but he said nothing.

In the thermopolis, or steam bath, the elephantine cock raised eyebrows and evoked whispers from the men sitting in a circle around the steaming stones.

Contus spied one man whose smile made the room lighter. They sat beside him. On closer inspection, they could see a caste in one eye rendering him partially blind.

The man extended a hand. "Kolossos." Neither Chrysion nor Contus knew much of the Macedonian tongue, but they were able to introduce themselves. Unlike the others in the room, Kolossos wore a towel. He repeated his name, then pointed to his crotch. He opened the towel, revealing a massive cock. A colossus, of course!

Chrysion asked in broken Macedonian, "Do you speak Thracian?"

"Thracian? I am from Thrace! Of course, I do!"

It was a relief to meet a countryman. He touched his giant cock and said, "Do you want to play?" He put a hand under Chrysion's buttocks and wiggled a finger into the loose hole.

Chrysion was startled by the man's boldness. Contus laughed and said, "I believe we have met the first church member."

The three men left the steam room, Contus grabbing a wooden rinsing bowl from the shower room. They went to the toilets, the darkest room in the bath, and Kolossos locked the door.

"We must stop if someone requires the toilet, but it's rare." They were in near darkness, for this room's only light source was candlelight from the hallway. With the door shut, the air was the color of squid ink.

Kolossos sat on a toilet seat, his enormous penis towering skyward. Chrysion sat on it, surprised by how thick it was. He wondered if he could take Contus at the same time. He chuckled. Of course, he could. He had devoted his ass to cock, and it would not suddenly lose its faith.

When Chrysion was settled in Kolossos's lap, Contus lifted his lover's legs towards the ceiling, exposing the hole he knew so well. It was tight, perhaps too tight. With great force, he pushed the swollen apple into his lover. Kolossos was deep in the second chamber. The passageway was cramped, but Contus found entry to the third chamber with great effort. He heard his lover cry out.

"Are you okay?"

Chrysion shook his head, but Contus couldn't see in the dark.

He repeated.

Chrysion spoke. "It hurts terribly, but I will heal."

"May I continue?"

"Yes. I need communion."

Contus became trapped in the third chamber. He could move back and forth, but the corona of his cock was like an arrowhead; it could not move in reverse past the huge thick cock of their fellow countryman. So Contus moved in small, rapid strokes.

"Oh! Oh! That is incredible!" Kolossos shivered with ecstasy. When Chrysion spasmed, he cried out. It was agony and pleasure in equal measure. There was no give; it was like a tree lodged in his entrails. When his innards contracted, they hurt.

Contus heard the signal. Chrysion panted like a dog on a hot day. Contus was so familiar with his lover that he caught his semen even in the pitch dark. He held the sweet liquid in front of Kolossos, who sipped it.

"Oh, that's sweet! Oh! Why does it tingle so?"

Contus said, "It's holy communion. First the boy, then the man."

"Whatever it is, I will soon lose my seed inside the boy."

Chrysion spoke between moans. "It won't be lost."

The boy's moans became pants, then a loud cry. Contus caught his lover's second flow, feeding it to their friend and Chrysion before lapping up the remains.

"Oh, for the love of cock! I'm going to blast inside you!" Kolossos was wedged so tightly there was no room for his seed to spill. It stretched the second chamber before finally bursting into the third.

Contus was able to move smoothly after that blast. Chrysion's entrails were slick with sperm, and Kolossos's tumescence had subsided slightly. Contus finished at the deepest point in his lover's gut, at the seventh rib.

A knock came at the door.

"One minute!" Kolossos tried to withdraw and couldn't. Contus had him pinned to the walls of Chrysion's chambers.

Contus grabbed the bowl and placed it beneath Chrysion's anus. Together, the two men pulled out. Kolossos's seed spilled out with his cock, and Contus's semen was quick to follow. The bowl filled with the endless load and threatened to overflow.

Another insistent knock. "It's urgent! Please hurry!"

Kolossos unlocked the door, letting in the light. The frustrated patron sat on a toilet and loudly shat. Contus rushed to Chrysion's side. His lover was doubled over, semen running from his ass.

The communion bowl overflowed with the divine host. Chrysion couldn't wait; he needed the healing power immediately. He skipped turns and drank a large helping from the bowl. He sighed. A thin trickle of blood ran down his leg.

Contus grabbed his lover by the arm. "Are you injured?"

"Nothing that communion won't heal."

Kolossos saw the bowl. "What is that for?"

"Communion. Healing. If you drink that, your eye will heal."

Kolossos frowned. "Blindness can't be healed."

Contus passed him the bowl. "Trust me."

Kolossos sipped the communion seed. "It is good!" He drank again. They passed the bowl until they were very full. Like drunkenness, but with visions, they became intoxicated on the solid brew. In the steam room, the tendrils of water licked the ceiling and formed ghostly shapes. Kolossos began to laugh and could not stop. "I feel as though I have smoked Asterion!"

For an hour, the men remained inebriated. They soaked in the hot bath water, jumped into the icy water, then soaked in tepid water. Kolossos and Contus drew much attention with their enormous genitals, while Chrysion attracted a different breed of man with his perfectly round butt and tiny penis. All who approached heard tell of the church forming in Thessaloniki. Kolossos would be the leader with his mighty cock and massive estate overlooking the harbor. The first meeting would be on the morrow at sundown.

CHAPTER 3

Kolossos insisted the two lovers stay with him. He had servants retrieve their horse and belongings from the inn while his cook prepared a seafood feast. After a fish and shrimp soup, smoked octopus, fried squid, sturgeon eggs, and roast sea bass landed on the table in courses. They drank heavily of the wine imported from Latium outside Rome. The meal was so delicious, Chrysion nearly wept, and he dabbed at his eyes with a linen napkin. When the meal had settled, the last course arrived: a delicate pastry made of hundreds of thin sheets of dough stuffed with honey, rose water, and walnuts.

Bellies distended, the men retired to their chambers and fell asleep.

In the morning, Kolossos gave the two lovers a tour of the estate. The villa consisted of a dozen large rooms surrounding a central courtyard. On the grounds were a large barn for horses, a ball court, a cooling shed, and a modest temple dedicated to Hermes. The temple was in the middle of an olive orchard.

Kolossos said, "These trees have many buds, but the

fruit will not be ready until the spring produces fruit and the summer sun ripens it. It is autumn, and the harvest is over."

Wide, cushioned benches lined the temple walls. A large stone table sat at the center. In the middle of the table was a marble statue of Hermes, with a proudly erect penis.

Kolossos said, "Hermes's temple will be perfect for this evening's worship."

And it was.

When evening came, dozens of men appeared for worship. Inside the temple, foods befitting an orgy adorned the central table. Inside the entrance stood the three men naked. First Kolossos, then Contus, then Chrysion. As the first man entered the temple, he knelt and kissed the two massive cocks, then Chrysion's beautiful behind. He touched a finger to his lips and then his forehead. The sight of this made all three men very hard. The next man had no need to kneel. He bent slightly to kiss Kolossos, stood straight to kiss Contus, then stooped to kiss the perfect behind of Chrysion. A tradition was born in those moments that may last for eons. The simple kiss of devotion upon entering the temple was simple, practical, and beautiful.

By the time the sun touched the horizon, each man had received twice a dozen kisses. The temple had nearly reached capacity on its very first day!

Contus addressed the assembly. "My cock is the source of the great seed, and the great seed is but one portion of the blessed communion. Chrysion's small, sweet seed is the fruit of the union and must be consumed for communion to be complete. Kolossos, your host, has been given holy communion, so his cock is now a permanent source of the great seed. We will find among you a novitiate with little length or girth; they will be your permanent source of sweet seed. Who offers their backside to Kolossos?

A young man, slender with brown hair and green eyes, stepped forward. "I am Teodoros, and I shall commune."

While men of all shapes and sizes stroked their cocks, Kolossos licked Teodoros's hole. Next, he stood, his cock at full mast, and pushed the head inside. The handsome novitiate cried out in agony. When his cries reduced to whimpers, Kolossos went further inside.

"Your hole resists my mighty cock. Shall I stop?"

Teodoros shook his head. "I am learning to accommodate you. Please continue."

While Kolossos trained his novitiate, Contus entered the blissful doorway between Chrysion's buttocks. He felt good to be with his beloved before a crowd. Chrysion moaned with pleasure. His hole was a wide hallway now and gave little resistance to the obscenely large cock of the demigod.

Kolossos buried himself to the hilt. Teodoros opened his mouth in a silent cry of joy. One by one, men stepped forward and fed their modest cocks to him and Chrysion. They erupted quickly, for such was the sexual energy in the temple that it echoed off the walls. Chrysion and Teodoros hungrily swallowed the seed and opened their mouths again for the next in line. In total, twenty members gave their sacred nectar to the two young men.

When all were sated, Contus and Kolossos filled the colons of the two novitiates. A member grasped an enormous fruit bowl from the center table, emptying it. The leader and the demigod then filled the vessel with the holy seed. Kolossos marveled at the volume of semen he had produced. It was tenfold the usual amount. But even with the demigod's bushel of sperm, the bowl was half-filled.

Kolossos clapped his hands. "We need each of you to spill communion seed in one of the catamites."

The men who fed the semen to the boys were required to produce more. Though they were of all ages and sizes, the reverberation of sexual power gave them a second wind. A gray-haired man stepped forward and entered Teodoros with ease. A man with jet black hair and a hairy chest produced an enormous erection and put it inside Chrysion. Kolossos added his cock beside that of the gray-haired man, and Contus joined the dark-haired man inside Chrysion. Each man whose cock came in contact with that of Kolossos or Contus became aware of a tingling sensation as the power of communion passed from cock to cock. Small bolts of lightning traveled up their spines when they came, making their heads grow heavy. They retired to a bench to recover.

The remaining men formed two lines - large cocks for Chrysion, average to small for Teodoros. The transfer of cock energy continued for several hours until every man was satisfied. Chrysion squatted over the bowl and emptied his bowels of the fruit of ten men's cocks. Teodoros did the same. Then at midnight, the bowl was passed from mouth to mouth as the First Phallic Church of Thessaloniki inaugurated its new temple with sacred communion.

Contus spoke: "Go forth, initiates, for as long as one High Priest and one Leader are present, you may pass the power to others. May the Phallic Brotherhood multiply in numbers."

But the festivities had only just begun. The semen's power granted sacred visions of ghostly apparitions, colored lights, and dragon's teeth. The men cleared the central table, and all willing catamites lay on their backs with their holes exposed. Men filled those holes with earthly flesh and Olympian semen. The orgy continued until the sun's first rays scraped the dawn sky. They produced much semen, not all of it making its way into bowls, for the orgy had spilled out of the temple into the olive orchard. Every last man had satisfied their primal lust.

CHAPTER 4

Kolossos, Contus, and Chrysion collapsed into a large bed to sleep off the night's excesses. They awoke that afternoon when a servant rushed into the room.

"Kolossos, sir, you must come see."

The two lovers and the wealthy merchant followed the servant to the orchard. To their astonishment, the trees bore bright green olives.

Kolossos was dumbstruck. "This miracle shall make me a wealthier man indeed!"

The seed spilled the previous night had passed its fertility and power into the orchard. From that day forward, all olive trees bore fruit in September and ripened by January.

"Surely I will share this knowledge with the worshippers so that they may spill their sacred seed in their own gardens."

Contus said, "It must be the seed of a catamite, spilled by pleasure alone, with no masturbation."

Kolossos stared at the phallic god. The cloud had disappeared from his eye. "How do you know this?"

Contus shrugged. "I don't know how; I just do."

The temple of Phallic Worship at Uskudama took seven seasons to establish, but here in Thessaloniki, it was already twenty members strong. In Thrace, the men were less interested in fucking boys, and their society looked down on the practice. Macedonia had a reputation for more liberal sexual freedom; men and boys lay with each other as a matter of course. Macedonian soldiers kept male lovers. Thus the church was ripe for establishment. Add to that the prosperity and fertility produced by the communion, and a cult was sure to form.

Over the next month, Kolossos hosted Saturday night orgies in the temple of Hermes. The semen from the catamites, produced without manual stimulation, was consumed for strength, health, and wealth. The remainder was so powerful that a single drop of communion semen spilled in a garden would yield a bountiful harvest. The legend of Contus Pedalis grew with each orgy. Hundreds of worshippers packed the temple until there was no room. Kolossos had a makeshift annex built to house the swelling crowd.

The worshippers had no book to guide them, so their stories of the power of Contus and Chrysion were whispered from ear to ear, growing wilder and more fantastic with each telling.

Chrysion overheard a novitiate saying, "Contus was born from the very cock of Zeus himself. His powers come from Mount Olympus."

A man with a long thin cock said, "I can thicken my pole by merely entering the ass of Chrysion."

A poet, short in stature and hung very small, said, "I want Contus inside me. He will make my headaches go away."

The poet's friend responded, "Any man with sufficient cock now carries the power of Contus. Lay with the first man you see."

The three founders of the church gathered in the main hall on a Sunday afternoon to discuss the chaotic growth of the cult of Contus Pedalis.

Contus said, "My guardians gave me a Roman name, but for the cult to thrive, it must be in a language that will last, such as the Athenian tongue."

It was true that Latin had produced few scholarly works, and Greek was the language of philosophers, poets, and mathematicians. Kolossos nodded his assent.

Chrysion said, "We can't just call it the Church of Cock; it will offend women and priests."

Kolossos agreed. "Pedalis means twelve inches, yet

you are so much larger than your name. Let us then call your cock by its measure. *Paykos* is a cubit, the measure of a man's arm from fingertip to elbow."

Contus said, "The temple of the cubit lacks something."

Chrysion said, "The cubit is sacred. *Hagia*."

Contus shook his head. "Hagiapaykus" is ugly.

Kolossos smiled. "What about *pria*? Beloved?"

Chrysion clapped his hands. "The Temple of Priapaykos!"

Kolossos shook his head. "In truth, I would say two cubits is more accurate, but *priabipaykos* is unpleasant to the ear, so why don't we instead just say a foot, just like your own last name? *Priapous* the beloved twelve inches."

Contus grinned. "I like it. No, I love it."

The next order of business was to write a holy book to outline the rules and beliefs of the worshippers.

"I volunteer, for I know how to write," said Chrysion. "I will begin with the fundamental rules of worship, but then I will also tell the story of Contus Pedalis and his sacred semen."

The three agreed that Chrysion should write the rules and the gospel of Priapous. The first high priest of the Temple of Priapous committed the rites to scrolls.

CHAPTER 5 - TEMPLE BYLAWS

The Temple is a community committed to recognizing the divinity of the phallus in all its forms. So, too, is the semen, the sacred covenant of communion between man and Priapous. Here are the sacred tenets:

1. Anywhere two or more men gather is the temple.
2. So long as one of the men has taken communion from another member of the temple, the union is sacred.
3. To worship, the man with the largest phallus must insert it into the hole of the smallest man.
4. Communion consists of three sexual acts: the insertion of the large phallus, the spontaneous ejaculation of the small phallus, and the spilling of the seed of the large phallus in the chambers of the smallest man.
5. Communion continues with the consumption of the seed. First, catch the semen of the smaller member in the palm of a large hand and drink thereof. Second, catch the seed of the large phallus by spilling it into a bowl, then drink therefrom.
6. The act of communion in large gatherings shall see the next largest member commune with the next smallest member.
7. Communion may be taken directly from the source via the act of oral worship.
8. Two large men may penetrate the smaller man when desired, thereby doubling the bounty.
9. Spilling seed is not forbidden but is wasteful.
10. For a smaller man to manually stimulate himself is allowed but is less sacred than spontaneous ejaculation.
11. At any gathering, the member of the temple with the largest phallus is the Leader, and the man with the smallest is the high priest.
12. A man shall be deemed small and engage as a catamite (passive) when his erection is not

      long enough for the entire head to pass the second ring of the anus.

13. A man shall be deemed large and engage as a pedicant (active) if the corona passes the second ring and fully enters the rectum.

14. A man shall be deemed sacred either if his cock be long enough to enter the second chamber or so short that he cannot use it for insertive sex.

15. Group worship shall take place Saturday nights in a location selected for its seclusion and capacity to hold a gathering.

16. Members of Temple Priapous may seek communion with other members at any time. See Tenet I

17. Because communion is sacred and open to all, members should avoid refusing communion with another member.

18. If one member refuses communion to another, the second man shall not force communion or retaliate against the first.

19. Members are comrades of the phallic brotherhood. As such, they shall treat one another with dignity and respect.

20. The erect phallus is a manifestation of the gods and a sign of their wisdom, grace, and generosity.

Kolossos hired a mason to carve the twenty tenets into a marble tablet, which he then placed on the temple's rear wall for all to read.

CHAPTER 6

Seasons passed. Saturday nights at the temple were always crowded to capacity with naked men, fucking and sucking to their hearts' content. The seed was gathered and distributed. Feeding it to one's bulls made many cows give birth. Sprinkling it in a vegetable patch would ensure a rich harvest. Men grew wealthy by soaking a coin in the semen. The bounty that Priapous promised was so attractive even the most pious man would set aside his beliefs for a night of debauchery and pleasure, knowing they would receive more than they gave.

One Saturday night, exhausted from the excesses of pleasure, Contus sat in the orchard upon a stone bench and rested. His serpentine cock hung from his groin, resting on the fertile soil. Chrysion, drunk on semen, sat on his lap, stroking the massive member. It rose from the ground and stretched skyward. Chrysion discovered he was ensnared in a cock trap that held him pinned to his beloved.

From a nearby olive branch came a familiar trill; it was the dove.

She sang:

> *In Saloniki, you have built*
> *A temple to the phallus*
> *That fills its faithful to the hilt*
> *And brings luck to the palace.*
>
> *But time moves on you must depart*
> *For elsewhere you shall nourish.*
> *Across the sea is Hellespont*
> *Where Priapous will flourish.*

And away flew the dove once again.

Kolossos learned of the message and grew despondent. He felt genuine love for both men, erotic, friendly, and familiar. To lose such friends would tie like cords around his heart. But he understood the campaign to establish the Temple of Priapous did not end in Thessaloniki.

Lying unclothed in his bed with the two lovers, he

said, "My dear friends, how can I bid thee adieu? My heart pains me to think of my bed empty once more."

Contus wiped away a tear. "As we once filled your bed, so too shall another."

Kolossos sighed. "I have fucked a thousand catamites but have only ever loved one." He looked at Chrysion and winked.

Chrysion smiled. "Teodoros has confided to me that he would gladly take my place by your side."

Teodoros, the first novitiate, was the first man Kolossos fucked after receiving his communion. He had a shapely bottom and a perfect tiny penis, one-tenth the size of Kolossos.

"Next Saturday, I shall seek him out and beat his innards with my club," said Kolossos.

Chrysion said, "Don't forget the gentle kisses and manly caresses. His bottom will thank you for showing mercy."

The men laughed.

Kolossos stood, his heavy member swinging between his legs. "I command a fleet of merchant ships. One shall take you to Hellespont to the port of Lampsacus, and I'll remain behind to spread the good news westward. From Lampsacus, you can reach all of Asia Minor and the Levant."

"I have a parting gift for you," said Chrysion. "I have communed directly with so many men that I have learned to open my mouth beyond limits. I wish to take communion from your loins as no one else has ever done."

Kolossos showed tumescence; his member grew and began its journey skyward. "You would do that for me?"

The boy nodded. "Nothing would make me happier." He knelt on the bed, his mouth at waist level. The fearsome cock, with its angry red head, hovered midair. Chrysion held the colossus with both hands to steady it. He clamped his mouth over the opening and unhinged his jaw. With ease, he took the fist-sized head into his mouth. Kolossos exhaled loudly.

Contus watched the communion unfolding, and he felt the familiar swelling between his legs. The enormous cock stretched and yawned as it lifted off the bed. Contus moved closer to his lover, so the hard head rested on Chrysion's backside.

"May I?"

Chrysion answered with mouth full. "Mmm."

Contus made his cock slick with olive oil, then pressed against the hole of the boy he loved, the only one who could ever take him. With slight pressure, he pushed past the gates into the first chamber. He rose to one knee to move into the second chamber. He walked forward on both knees, holding Chrysion by the waist to keep him steady. He reached the third chamber as his pubic mound came to rest on the ample buttocks.

Chrysion was taking communion at both ends. It excited him so much that he shuddered, achieving orgasm effortlessly. Contus put a big hand under the boy's tiny penis and caught the flow. He fed it to Kolossos, then the boy, and took the last bit himself.

Kolossos shed tears of joy. "I never thought I would know this feeling. How grateful I am to have it once in this life!"

The demigod felt the familiar churn of Chrysion's innards. It felt like a thousand tiny hands were stroking his cock from stem to stern. "By the gods, Chrysion, you were delivered to me. I thank each of them. Oh!" The waves of contraction grew more intense so that the thousand hands joined together to become five hundred, then two hundred fifty, then fifty, then 25, then 10, and at last, the waves came together in a single intense stroke that ran the entire length of Contus's mighty cock.

"I cannot last long!"

Kolossos got another huge surprise. Chrysion

grabbed him by the buttocks and pulled him to him, letting the huge cock slide down his throat. He bobbed up and down, holding his breath, keeping the monster lodged in his throat, but stroking it with his gullet.

"By all the gods, Chrysion, never have I felt such pleasure!" Kolossos began fucking the boy's throat. He withdrew enough to give him breath, then plunged back down. "It's better than any cunt or ass. Ohhh!"

Contus, meanwhile, was at the precipice. "I cannot hold it any longer. Uhhh!" With that, he flooded Chrysion's bowels with his manly fluid.

Kolossos could hear the raging river flow from Contus, which put him over the edge. "Oh, gods! I'm coming!" Chrysion pulled him close, so the endless flow of semen bypassed the boy's mouth and flowed straight to his stomach.

As always, Chrysion became so ecstatic from sex that his penis spat out another helping of high priest communion, which they shared all around.

Kolossos softened, but Chrysion clung to the enormous cock, nursing its final drops. At last, he let the beast go, and it smacked Kolossos loudly on the lower thigh.

The wash basin caught the huge ejaculation as it flowed from Chrysion's bum. All three men drank to their fill, but much was still left. Rather than see it go to waste, they went to the citrus grove and scattered it among the lemon trees. Blossoms appeared instantly.

GOSPEL OF PRIAPUS BOOK
THREE

Being the account of a perilous journey, the march to Lampsacus, the conversion of the Centurions, and the elevation of Priapus and Chrysion to immortal gods in the wood and fruit of the fig tree.

CHAPTER 1

The next morning, the two lovers gathered their belongings and followed Kolossos to the port. There they saw great vessels unloading spices from the Indus and bolts of fabric from silken Samarkand. Kolossos navigated the busy harbor with the confidence befitting a powerful merchant.

A sun-baked man called out, "Ho! Kolossos! 'Tis I, Damian!"

He approached with a broad smile, one hand outstretched.

They shook hands, demonstrating that they were equals under Hellenic democracy. Damian wore a tunic that had only one sleeve. His right nipple was exposed, and he wore a ring in it, which excited Chrysion greatly. His excitement did not go unnoticed by the handsome captain. He patted the boy on his rump and said, "May ye open to my bidding, lad." It was friendly chatter, but it bore a menace beneath the smile.

Kolossos grew melancholy. "Here is where I bid ye farewell, dear comrades." He opened his powerful arms wide and welcomed both men in his wide embrace. He kissed Chrysion's hair and Contus's lips. "Damian will care for your every need, and I have paid him well."

Damian gave a mischievous smile. "Aye, that you did, Kolossos." He put an arm around the two men. "My most precious cargo."

Kolossos wiped a tear and waved farewell.

Contus was far too innocent to detect what Chrysion had. Damian was without conscience. He was untrustworthy. But Kolossos had chosen him out of his whole fleet, so he must be good at his job. Or so they believed.

Damian steered the two lovers away from their dear friend towards his ship. "Here she is. This is Niki."

He pointed to the impressive vessel with 90 oar holes per side.

Chrysion marveled at the size. "It's so big!"

Damian grabbed his crotch and waggled his cock under the tunic. "That's what the ladies say. And the boy-whores too." He frowned when neither laughed at his joke. "The hold is filled with Amphorae of Olive Oil, Wool, and Oregano. Bound for Rodos."

Chrysion frowned. "Rodos? That is not on the way to Lampsacus."

Damian snarled. "Kolossos paid me well but not well enough to give up my trade. We will gather cargo in Rodos bound for Lampsacus."

Contus opened his mouth to speak, but Chrysion squeezed his hand and shook his head softly. The ensuing silence gave discomfort to all three.

The ship raised its sails and pulled away from the port. Chrysion had the urge to jump overboard, but he knew it was too late. To confirm his fears, he said, "Where do we sleep?"

"With the other slaves!"

Contus said, "Slaves? Whatever do you mean?"

"I mean, you're locked in the hold, and you won't see full daylight until I'm finished with the both of you."

He pushed Contus down the stairs. Chrysion ran after, but Damian grabbed him by the neck. "Not yet. I have more for you!"

He picked up the small youth and carried him to his cabin, throwing him roughly on the bed. "You know what comes next."

"Face or Buttocks?" Chrysion's former life as a paid catamite would serve him well in these moments."

"Let me see that beautiful behind." The sailor roughly grabbed the tunic and lifted it. He spread the cheeks and tasted the hole.

"Have you been lying with horses? Why is this so loose?"

Chrysion realized at that moment that his lover's big secret had escaped Damian's eye. A man like Damian thought only of his own cock and had no cause to notice another.

"I was a catamite in Istambolia. The men there are rather large."

When Damian pulled out his hard cock, it was a relief. It was short and narrow. "Perhaps the mouth will be tighter." And indeed, he meant mouth, for his penis could not reach the throat.

The sailor grabbed Chrysion by the ears and shoved his cock into the pretty mouth. Chrysion knew well the trick to make any man feel bigger. He tightened his lips and pretended to gag.

"Do you enjoy my cock in your mouth?"

Chrysion nodded. It was mostly a lie. He tasted salt on his tongue, a signal that this seafaring rogue was near orgasm. Reaching up a hand, Chrysion tugged on the nipple ring.

"Oh, gods, that feels great!" Damian threw his head back and roared.

A small helping of sperm filled Chrysion's mouth. Damian watched him closely. "You'd best not spit that out, boy. Swallow it."

It had been many moons since Chrysion had tasted unconsecrated sperm, and it was bitter. He forced the milky brew down his throat, gagging for real this time.

Damian had no pretense of passion, love, or care. He escorted Chrysion to the hatch and pushed him. Chrysion nearly lost footing as he went into the inky gloom.

"I expect you'll provide me service again. Be prepared."

CHAPTER 2

As Chrysion's eyes adjusted to the darkness, he spat to remove the acrid taste from his mouth.

"Chrysion?" He heard his lover calling from a nearby bunk. He followed the voice to Contus.

"What did he do to you?"

Chrysion shrugged. "Nothing that hasn't been done to me many times."

"We have to share a bunk, and it's cramped." Contus showed him the hard wood that formed their bread. Chrysion took the pack with their belongings and removed a large wool blanket.

Contus hopped down, and the two folded the blanket to fit the space. It was much softer. They made a pillow of their winter tunic made of soft, thick cotton yarn.

"It's still very tight. Can we both fit?"

Chrysion smiled. "We'll gain much space if you fuck me to sleep and leave it in."

Such language excited Contus; his member began to swell. Chrysion lay atop it.

"Sorry, but we must keep this a secret. Damian is a loose hinge, and he will take your size as a great insult."

"With your body so close to mine, I fear it won't go down."

There were nearly two hundred slaves that shared the quarters with them. Many spoke strange tongues from the Levant, Egypt, or Libya; others were from Dacia, Gallia, and other far-flung provinces of the Roman Empire. But one slave, old and infirm, spoke the tongue of Anatolya.

"Friends, fortune has brought you to me. For three long years, I have been unable to speak my mother tongue, and to hear it from your lips is music indeed."

Chrysion extended a hand and introduced himself and his lover.

The old man said, "I am Ibrahim. I'm grateful for your presence."

"And I you," said Chrysion.

Ibrahim beamed. "Such a beautiful visage you have. So, too, does your friend Contus."

Contus smiled. "Thank you. I rarely get compliments on my face."

Chrysion squeezed his hand to remind him of the secret.

Ibrahim leaned in close. "I overheard you. Please know that your big secret is safe with me. And you're right to believe that Damian would be jealous. But I am curious to see it all the same."

Chrysion said, "When it is safe to do so, you will see it."

Ibrahim gave the lovers a tour of the floating prison named Niki. The living quarters were in the center of the ship, while the outer portion consisted of rows of benches and long oars.

"We are in high winds now, but between here and

Rodos, there may be doldrums. We will break our backs in those still waters.

At the ship's rear were toilets arranged in a semi-circle with no door. Several men were shitting in plain sight, speaking a strange tongue.

One of the men shouted at Ibrahim, and Ibrahim called back in the strange tongue and laughed.

"Those men are Trojans. Soldiers who lost their freedom in wars with Sparta and Athens."

Contus looked at their new friend. "What did they say to you?"

Ibrahim laughed. "They told me to paint a portrait of them sitting upon the commode so I won't stare any longer, and I returned the insult by saying it was only worthy of a love poem."

Chrysion asked, "How many languages do you speak?"

Ibrahim rubbed his chin. I don't know the count, but I speak six well enough to jest. There are maybe twenty others I know enough to get by.

Ibrahim next led them to the dining area at the front of the ship.

"We are treated as horses. They give us only enough fuel to row: bread, olive oil, and sheep cheese. They feed us sausage at the solstice and the equinox but no wine. I have gone far too long without wine."

Contus smiled. "I can produce a drink more intoxicating than wine and more fortifying than sausage."

Chrysion spoke. "Ibrahim, I have been jailed once. In jail, every man finds a mate. Have our fellow slaves found love in this manner?"

Ibrahim nodded. "We come from many places. Most believe that there is shame in being a bottom or catamite. So we have very few couples. Ten very busy young men accommodate the needs of the rest."

Chrysion put together pieces of a puzzle. "Are there men who wish to stay here on the ship?"

Ibrahim shook his head. "No one wishes to stay."

"Are any loyal to Damian or his crew?"

Ibrahim thought hard. "There are three young catamites who serve his needs, and he grants them special favors. Are you planning something?"

Chrysion shrugged. "Contus and I are in service to man. We raise the spirit through communion. It is powerful medicine."

"Communion? Eat in union...what is that?"

"We eat together. The body and the blood of the demigod in our midst. But before doing such things, we must know it will remain a secret from the captain and crew."

Ibrahim hopped from one foot to another. "I will make it my task to swear every last slave to secrecy. If one refuses, we will tie him to the center mast."

A bell rang. "It's time for our meal. Come."

CHAPTER 3

The three sat at a long table surrounded by many men of all shapes, sizes, colors, and countries. At their table were the Persians and Egyptians at opposite ends, and Dacians sat in the middle. Ibrahim engaged each group in their own language, letting them know of the great miracle among them and swearing them to secrecy. The three groups complied. Ibrahim left their table and went to a small table where only young men dined. These catamites all spoke a blended tongue of Athenian and Roman. Ibrahim gestured carefully and studied the faces of the young men. He spent more time with three whom Chrysion assumed were favorites of Damian. They looked somewhat like him; all were fair-haired and small in stature.

Ibrahim returned to the table. "I think we can trust all but one catamite. Not Iulian, the Dacian. He is loyal only to Damian."

Chrysion said, "Does he know what we are planning?"

Ibrahim shook his head. "I had to test first to see where loyalties lay. I made no mention of the secret to any of them."

Meal time came to an end. There were approximately twenty men who would cooperate, nine who seemed likely, and one who would cause problems, Iulian of Dacia.

Contus watched his lover and Ibrahim strategize. He was too pure to understand how men require manipulation to comply. His knowledge of politics was almost nil.

The few rays of sunlight that lit the slaves' quarters vanished. The moonlight was a poor light source, and there were no candles or lanterns. It was time for rest.

Contus climbed into the bunk first. It was so dark nobody could see what they did next. Chrysion rubbed the head of Contus's cock until it rose to his chest. Chrysion sat on Contus's shoulder and took the massive cock inside him. He had to change positions as the cock turned corners, but at long last, it was wedged solidly inside him, near the ribs. Chrysion turned his head and planted his lips on Contus's. In rhythmic waves, Chrysion moved his bottom, using his insides to stroke his lover's enormous cock.

"Oh, that feels good, Chrysion."

Chrysion said, "It does."

In this way, the fair-haired youth brought his lover toward orgasm in slow, gentle strokes. As free men, they were rough and quick with their sexual union. But here, in the blackness of night, surrounded by two hundred slaves, they were forced to move slowly. Chrysion held his hand to his belly, where he felt the giant log of flesh moving inside him. Contus felt the pressure, and it excited him. He increased the speed of his strokes, stretching the third chamber as more blood filled his member. The waves of muscle contractions began, bringing both men closer to orgasm.

Chrysion panted. "I'm there." Contus caught the sweet semen in his hand, fed it to his lover, and then ate the rest. Chrysion's taste and fragrance were a direct link to Aphrodite. Contus's cock swelled and stretched, filling the youth completely while wave after wave rocked his slender body until he ejaculated again. The second dose of semen was the tipping point for Contus, who could no longer retain his seed. The slow sex had caused him to stretch so deep and wide that his semen couldn't stay in the third chamber and flowed into the fourth.

Chrysion spoke. "We'll have to wait until morning to release the communion from my bowels."

Bound together by the huge cock, the lovers drifted into sleep.

CHAPTER 4

The following day, Chrysion retrieved a wash basin from their bag. He had packed it for the journey, not knowing if such things existed on ships. Perhaps they did, but not in the slave quarters. In the tight space, it was hard for the two lovers to separate and catch the flow in the basin, but they managed. The basin only filled halfway, as Chrysion's body had absorbed much of the communion. What came out was thicker than usual, like porridge, and very easy to eat with their fingers. As slaves passed by on their way to the toilets, they spied the strange couple eating porridge from a giant bowl. Contus grew a thick beard after eating the concentrated semen.

There were no bathing facilities in the slaves' quarters, but enough sea water entered through small holes, filling buckets. Men were able to wash themselves with their hands. Contus was afraid to show himself, but

Ibrahim reassured him. Iulian always sees Damian in the cuddy after he showers. There he is now.

Ibrahim nodded in the direction of a young man with long brown hair, no beard or body hair, and a plump bottom.

Iulian dressed and whistled for one of the crew to escort him above deck. When he was gone, Ibrahim jumped on a table and shouted in vulgar Latin, which could be understood or translated by many slaves.

"Fellow slaves! We have among us a god. Before the helmsman and his musicians arrive, let me tell you of our impending freedom! None of us should remain in bondage, but we are weak and malnourished. They don't give us the beans that any ship would give. Are you hungry?"

The oarsmen looked from one to the other in puzzlement.

Ibrahim repeated, "I can't hear you! Are you hungry?"

"Yes!" a handful of oarsmen shouted.

"No one else? Are you hungry?"

Now the cabin filled with a resounding shout. "Yes!"

"Well, gentlemen, I have food for your body and soul. When you partake in it, you will grow stronger. And as a unit, we can overthrow this illegal slaver and his wretched ship!"

A Phoenician slave shouted, "What is this food you speak of?"

Ibrahim smiled. "I'm glad you asked, sir. It's the nectar of the gods, or of one god, to be precise. And you will see its source, for he lives among us and has come to save us all."

Contus disrobed and showered himself with the cold seawater. The men crowded around, gasping and pointing in amazement.

"Surely he is a god, the son of Zarathustra himself!" said one Babylonian.

"Nay, he is Zeus's offspring!" a Macedonian argued.

The oarsmen quibbled amongst themselves. Ibrahim stood tall. "He is a god unlike any other. He belongs to no other god, nor is he a single god of the Israelites. Worship him, and your crops will grow. Commune of his seed and your bodies will strengthen. Welcome him into your hearts, and you will have freedom."

The ship's hatch opened, and Paleos, the helmsman, descended with his piper and singer. Contus threw on his tunic, covering his magic pole.

"The winds are unfavorable. We will row to Rodos."

Paleos saw the men gathered in a vast circle around one man. "What is this?"

Ibrahim hopped down from the table. "We were certain there would be rowing today, so we chanted to raise our energy levels. Having no beans to fuel our bodies, we are sorely in need of courage."

The helmsman nodded. "You show good initiative, men. I agree; you should be fed and given rest. Not only because it makes my work all the more difficult but also for the shame it brings this ship to treat men so. Slavery is not a democratic institution."

Ibrahim translated for the men.

An Egyptian asked, "Is he with us?"

Ibrahim held a finger to his lips.

The piper and singer stood at the helm. The aulos flute played a lively tune, and the singer started to chant in a dialect no one understood, but all obeyed. For as his song gathered speed, the oars moved faster, too. The work was painful and exhausting. There were 170 oars and 200 men. They moved in and out in shifts of 30.

When Chrysion and Contus received respite, they nearly collapsed. They leaned on each other for support, then moved to the back of the ship and lay on their bunks. There was neither water nor food. Nor was there any place where they could take communion to rebuild their strength. No sooner had they regained their breath when they were called back to the oars for many more hours of grueling labor. The rowing continued for several days. Nobody was permitted to sleep for more than a few minutes. In this way, they could not celebrate communion on the open sea.

CHAPTER 5

Rodos is a distant island, far south and far east of Thessaloniki. They could be there in four days with favorable winds assisting the oars. On the fourth day, the ship passed under the Colossus and into the harbor at Rhodes.

The slaves remained below decks, locked in their quarters. Ibrahim gathered the slaves and began the complex process of organizing men for communion. The ten catamites were to serve 190 men, which would take too long. So, more men volunteered as hosts to receive communion in their holes, whether mouth or anus.

The ceremony began with Contus and Chrysion. One by one, the most well-endowed members of the rowing crew, many quite impressive, joined their cocks with Contus inside Chrysion, then drank the sweet nectar from the boy's tiny penis and the meal that spilled from his ass. These men were then free to go to the next catamite, with whom one would pedicate, and the other would irrumate, and in this way, communion spread from man to man. The entire crew, including fair-haired Iulian of Dacia, were in this way initiated into the cult of Priapous. Immediately, the men felt their muscles grow more substantial and their cocks grow harder. The ceremony concluded with passing the bowl of Contus's semen that had spilled from Chrysion's backside. From one man to the next, each took but a small sip, which was enough to send a jolt of god-like energy through their weary bodies.

With the power of the Priapic god at their heels, the men stormed the hold, forcing the iron bars out of their wooden frames. Two hundred angry men spilled onto the top deck. The ship was in the harbor, and the free sailors were away on shore leave. Only Paleos, the helmsman, the chanter, and the piper were left to watch the ship.

Upon seeing an angry mob break through the hold, he sat in prayer, holding his knees to his chest. The men were not angry with him. Ibrahim put a reassuring hand on his shoulder. "Brother, it is your choice; take communion with us and join us or disembark. We are setting sail for freedom."

Paleos stood, unsure of what was meant by the choice Ibrahim gave. "You are leaving? How is it that you broke through the iron bars?"

Ibrahim explained communion. Paleos shook his head in disbelief. "If I hadn't just witnessed you destroy your prison gates, I would doubt you. But surely a miracle is taking place."

At that moment, Contus approached. "Salve, Paleos."

The helmsman saw the outline of Contus's two-cubit pole swinging in his tunic. He smiled. "I will take communion."

Paleos unfastened his breeches and let them drop to the deck. His penis was astonishingly large, given the man's short, bulky frame.

Chrysion said, "You can use any of the catamites for your pleasure, and that will constitute communion."

Paleos looked him right in the eye and responded. "I have lusted for you since you first set foot on this ship."

Chrysion held up a finger in protest. "I am reserved for Contus. You would have to share me."

"Then so shall it be."

Contus filled his lover with his immense, powerful cock, then lay down to allow Paleos entry. The helmsman entered with considerable effort, and Chrysion cried out in pain.

"Have I hurt you, son?" Paleos put a reassuring paw on the boy's back.

Chrysion nodded. "It is only temporary. It will soon become joy. Press on."

And in that way, Paleos was indoctrinated into the Priapic Brotherhood. He ate of Chrysion's seed and then drank from the large bucket that filled with Contus's and his semen. They passed the bucket around.

The chanter was well-endowed, but the piper was tiny. With Chrysion's guidance, Paleos passed along the communion to those two. The piper put the chanter's "flute" in his mouth, and Paleos deposited his issue in the piper.

Ibrahim, a naturally gifted orator, stood on the prow and proclaimed. "We are free citizens. We are a church. Let us commandeer this ship and make for the Hellespont! First by water, then by land."

The crowd cheered. The men untied the ship and steered it out of the harbor under the massive legs of the Colossus. The vessel would be apprehended in open waters if they went straight across the bay to the nearest port. They decided to land at Physkos and follow the Roman roads to Lampsacus in the Hellespont.

In Physkos, Ibrahim negotiated the sale of the vessel to a local merchant.

CHAPTER 6

In each city or village they passed, the men took communion and shared the potent effluence with the local farmers. In this way, they found protection in each town they passed, and the cult of Priapous grew.

Farmers and merchants all wished to take communion, thereby increasing their crops and the value of their wares. Arriving in a town by nightfall, Ibrahim negotiated the barns and boarding houses for all the escaped slaves with the promise of bountiful crops by dawn. Indeed, the men took communion and scattered the remainder over the vines, roots, and trees that grew there. When the farmers saw the miracle of the holy seed, they converted immediately. In this way, the Temple of Priapous found new members throughout Ionia and Aeolis.

As the men brought the good news, so, too, did the Roman consuls learn of the new religion forming, worshipping a living god. This new religion was a threat to their power and status. As the cult moved closer to Lampsacus, the Empire gathered forces to take siege at Lampsacus when the followers of Priapous arrived.

The two hundred men had grown to five hundred when they arrived at the fortified city of Smyrna, a week's journey from Lampsacus. Two towering hunks of muscle stood watch at the gate when they approached. They were immovable and spoke not when spoken to.

Ibrahim did his best to speak sense into their heads, but they were as still as stone. A voice called down from the parapet above.

"You shall never find peaceful conversation with these warriors. Their minds follow a program after many years of training. Beware, they are dangerous."

Ibrahim called up to the man. "Perhaps you can help us gain entrance, for the night is near, and we have much good news to share with the fine people of Smyrna."

The man descended and opened a small window in the massive drawbridge. He whispered to avoid the guards from overhearing. "There is an entrance used only by merchants and vendors. It is a thousand cubits to the west." He pointed to a distant corner of the wall.

"Knock first three, then one, then three again. In that manner, you shall gain entrance, even though your numbers may be great."

Inside the great city's walls, the former slaves marveled at the splendor of the great marketplace. There were tens of thousands living here, rivaling anything Chrysion or Contus had seen. Not even Istambolia was so magnificent. The five hundred acolytes sat in the syntagma, or town square, while the three leaders searched for farmers with whom to bargain. They wandered the narrow streets, seeing no sign of fields or flowers.

Contus stopped a gentleman in the street. "Where are the farms?"

The man laughed. "This is a town of seafaring merchants. We get our meat, vegetables, milk, and eggs from vendors, and we deal in gold, silver, and lead." He held up three coins to illustrate.

Ibrahim stepped in. "Here, put your three coins in this pot, and they will multiply."

The man named Jonah laughed. "I'm no fool. You'll run off with the jar and my money."

"No, sir," said Ibrahim, "You will hold the jar. I promise you will only gain from this."

The man took the jar, dropped in the coins, and covered the pot with a lid.

"Now shake it a few times." He did as he was told. Upon opening the jar, he gasped, for his money had doubled. "How is this done?"

Ibrahim gestured to Contus. "He is a minor god, and his cock issues magic seed that brings plenty."

Contus lifted his tunic to show the gargantuan cock between his legs.

"What can I do to have more?"

Ibrahim was clever. "You must tell only men who wish to have wealth and plenty. Go forth in the marketplace and spread the word. We meet at sundown in the temple of Mercury."

Jonah agreed to spread the word. He paused. "Is this related to your temple?" He withdrew a necklace, from which was hanging a winged phallus.

Chrysion said, "Where did you get that?"

Jonah smiled. "They came on a fast ship from Physkos and are good luck charms for crops, cattle, fertility, and maritime commerce."

Ibrahim scoured the marketplace, buying every flying phallus he could find, seeing an opportunity to provide a symbol to the newly formed religion. He returned to the town square and distributed them among the former slaves, reserving many more for new recruits.

The amphitheater on the edge of the town lay dormant. It was not yet summer, and the tragedies and comedies were on hiatus. The five hundred men wandered the city streets, spreading the good news of the mighty phallus of Contus Pedalis and giving a winged penis to anyone who agreed to attend the ceremony.

That night, in addition to the five hundred acolytes, several hundred citizens of Smyrna attended communion. At the appointed hour, they disrobed and began the joyful union that transmitted the power of Contus to everyone present. When fellowship ended, there were over seven hundred followers of the faith, consecrated with sperm.

The congregant brought the sperm to the harbor, where they applied it to the prow of each merchant ship. With two hundred residents of Smyrna to spread the news, it would soon become a maritime power to rival Athens or Rome.

CHAPTER 7

The five hundred departed the following day, hoping to reach Lampsacus, the prophesied seat of the religion. They encountered Roman centurions on the path a day's journey south of Lampsacus near the ruins of the ancient kingdom of Troy.

"Ho! Who is this band of travelers? What business have you on the Roman road?"

Ibrahim spoke frankly. "We're followers of Priapus, the god of fertility, abundance, and crops."

The Head Centurion, Marcellus, grabbed Ibrahim and threw him in chains. The other soldiers surrounded as many members of the temple as they could.

Marcellus said, "We have orders from the Emperor himself to end this blasphemous cult. You dare put gods forward before Mercury, Apollo, Jove, or Minerva? You'll end your days in chains."

Ibrahim was undaunted. "Sir, if you but see the miracle of the cock of Contus Pedalis, you may feel its power and be swayed to join us."

"Abandon my post for a false god? I think not!"

The other soldiers began to put the members in chains. Contus stood on a rock and lifted his tunic. "Behold, this cock comes from Mount Olympus itself. Can you not see its god-like stature?"

Marcellus paused. The other soldiers grew slack-jawed.

Ibrahim added, "One drop of his sperm will make you a rich man. You'll have no need to serve an Emperor for small coins when you can have gold."

The sight of such an enormous cock was powerful. The soldiers began whispering amongst themselves.

Marcellus said, "How does it work?"

Contus stepped forward. "Put a hand here, and you'll feel the power of my cock."

Marcellus touched the mighty phallus and trembled. "It's true! There's power here. How may I know it?"

Seven of the thirty centurions were large enough to enter the second chamber. Marcellus was the largest, so he went first. One by one, they spilled their seed inside Chrysion and drank of his semen, adding their own to that of Contus. The other twenty-three soldiers reluctantly bent at the waist and allowed the top members of their legion to penetrate them and share in communion. Contus emptied his bowels of the holy seed into Marcellus's helmet, and all shared the nourishing brew. Although it was only one helmet, miraculously, it provided enough sustenance for the five hundred and thirty men.

Drunk on sperm, Marcellus swooned and sat on a stone. "I feel better than I have since my youth. Truly there is power in the sperm."

Ibrahim was still in cuffs. "Will you release me, kind sir?"

Marcellus produced a key and unchained his prisoner. "I will accompany you to Lampsacus, where several hundred soldiers are waiting to capture you."

So the raggedy band of sperm-eaters marched alongside their guardian Roman soldiers, reaching the outskirts of Lampsacus before sundown the next day.

Until the conversion at Smyrna, Contus's spiritual power had gone unnoticed by the gods on Mount Olympus. After so many men switched alliances to their new god, the god of cock, Zeus and his court were greatly upset. They had put a favorable wind to the backs of the Centurions, meddling in human affairs to correct the perceived imbalance. Still, the Centurions fell in worship of the almighty phallus. So, Diana filled her quiver with charmed arrows and stalked the great Contus Pedalis, now called Priapus, determined to end his reign. The day Contus marched into Lampsacus, the townspeople flocked to his side.

"The day of prophecy is here! The day we make a god of a man." The town's women prepared a mighty feast to feed the hungry horde. After the slaves and soldiers ate their fill, they gathered in the great temple that the townsmen had erected shortly after Contus's birth in expectation of the prophecy that one day he would return to found a mighty church.

Many men had taken the sacred communion already, and the orgy began with little planning. Contus mounted his lover, filling him to the ribs with his massive cock. Chrysion moaned with delight. "Contus, your love is greater than even your cock. I feel it in me, on me, and around me."

Contus kissed his young lover on the lips. "I will love you for eternity."

Centurions with giant cocks plowed men with mere nipples between their legs. Everywhere, seed spilled. Basins caught the holy communion, and the men shared it.

Chrysion felt the immense power of his lover in his belly. His waves of orgasm stroked the mighty cock of Priapus. When he spilled his seed, Chrysion fed it to his lover. When he came a second time, Contus threw his head behind him and roared, flooding Chrysion with more semen than ever before. It was so much it ran from his bottom past the colossal cock and into the basin below.

"I love you, Chrysion."

"And I love you."

CHAPTER 8

These vows of love were the last words of Contus and Chrysion. As they pledged their love, Diana, hiding in the rafters, released an arrow, piercing Contus through the waist and passing into the belly of Chrysion. At that moment, Contus turned to wood. His cock was the trunk of a mighty fig tree, and Chrysion became the fruit. The congregation wept and gnashed their teeth, seeing their god turned to wood and his beloved vessel turned to figs.

They passed the last bowl of his communion and poured the remainder on the fallow fields of grain that hadn't produced a surplus in many years. That year, the harvest was elevenfold what it had been years prior.

Diana's arrow only killed the mortal flesh of the two lovers. Their legacy, the holy communion of sacred sperm, lived in the towns where it was first spilled and spread to many towns far and wide. At Pompeii in Magna Grecia, the cult took hold so completely that it angered even Vulcan, who so rarely paid attention to the affairs of man. He destroyed that city and many sur-rounding towns to wipe out the cult of Priapus. But it has endured, taking many forms.

It is said that any thief stealing from a field guarded by a wooden carving of Priapus will feel his wrath. Such a thief, if young, Priapus will penetrate in the night. If the thief has a beard, Priapus will force himself into the man's mouth, thereby choking him to death. Even women who steal will feel their wombs ripped apart by the almighty cock that only Chrysion could endure. If the thief steals figs, they will surely die, for they are taking Chrysion from Contus. The wrath will be tenfold.

Just as Contus protected the slaves aboard the ship, oarsmen and sailors alike wear the phallus around their neck and eat figs before setting out to sea. The old gods grew weak, but Priapus lived on. When the son of the Hebrew God spread his gospel, it was accepted by many. The followers of Priapus saw no reason to give up the living god who had blessed their crops, so they wel-comed the son into their hearts but kept their cocks and holes in service to their erect, wooden god.

The cult of Priapus thrived and spread to many men

around the known world. The fig tree at Lampsacus still bears fruit all year long. The fruit of the tree has the unusual property of shrinking the penis of any man who eats it, making them a perfect vessel for communion. Whomsoever wears a branch from the tree in his belt will see his cock grow enough to reach the second chamber. For that reason, the tree remains hidden in a cloister for protection. The guardians of the tree will instruct any visitors on the proper means of conducting communion. As a result, many Priapic temples have appeared in cities of the old world and the new.

So ends the tale of Chrysion Bipenna and Contus Pedalis, no longer mortal men but deities.

III

ONE ETERNAL DAY

The Athens sun pierced the crack in my curtains, hit the mirror above the dresser, and shone directly on my face. I was staying at the Hotel Grande Bretagne on Syntagma Square. My flight from Los Angeles lasted 24 hours, 34 if you count the time difference. I made plane changes in New York City and London. I arrived in the late afternoon at my hotel and fell into a deep sleep that lasted thirteen hours.

A few moments after the sun disturbed my endless rest, there was a gentle knock at the door. I remembered I had ordered breakfast at dawn so I could explore Athens for a full day. I was in Greece on business and wouldn't have much free time after that day.

During the night, I had shed my clothes. The air conditioning was an afterthought in this 19th-century luxury hotel. One window had a loud evaporative cooler that only made the sweltering room damp and humid. I leaped out of bed to answer the door, forgetting that I was as naked as a newborn. I opened the door to find a very startled room service waiter. He stammered in his best English.

"Sir, uh, where shall I put the tray." His eyes darted downward, then widened.

I am hung like a horse, in case you didn't know, and the beast between my legs was rising with the morning. I suddenly realized my clothes were kicked about on the floor. I grabbed the napkin from his tray and held it at a diagonal. It was not enough to cover me, but it offered a modicome of modesty.

I glanced at the waiter's wedding ring and blushed. I had made this poor man look at my monstrous manhood. I knew he'd feel inadequate when he went home to his wife. It would take a week for him to get over it. I have a vivid imagination.

"Sorry about that. Please put it on the writing desk."

He bowed his head, rushed into my room, deposited the tray, and left without waiting for a tip. My dick got me into a lot of trouble, so I was grateful that it had just saved me a dollar. It was a double-edged sword of enormous proportions.

I devoured my full English with the enthusiasm of a war orphan. I hadn't eaten since the breakfast on the last leg of my journey.

Still naked, my cock bobbing from knee to knee, I looked for my suitcase, only to remember that the airline had misplaced it in London. I had only a small travel bag containing toiletries and a stack of brochures to hand out at the travel convention.

I looked at my sweaty, wrinkled suit and shrugged. The hotel concierge had promised to hound the airline until they brought my bags to him personally, but he said it might take a day or two. I worried I would have to go to the conference disheveled and unkempt. Worse things had happened.

I showered, washing away 34 hours of sweat and airplane dust. I took the usual care to clean under my foreskin, which gets pretty ripe without a daily shower. My balls are enormous, but they look small next to my dick. I washed under them, sniffing my finger and inhaling the musky brew before I applied soap. That smell, even my own, always made my dick hard. I was determined to rub one out in the shower, but another knock at the door disturbed my onanistic reverie.

"Who is it?"

"Room service again. Sorry, sir."

I wrapped the rather small white towel around my waist. It did nothing to hide my shamefully huge penis. I opened the door, dripping wet.

"Oh, sorry, sir. I really am. I forgot to have you sign this."

He presented a slip with the charge for the breakfast. He handed me a pen, and I signed. I saw him staring below my waist. Sometimes, even married men get curious.

"I can take a picture if it will help."

He didn't speak enough English to get my sarcasm.

He stood immobile, staring mercilessly. "I'm sorry, sir, I don't understand."

I saw his hand twitch. I knew that signal from a thousand encounters. He wanted to touch me.

It was pure fate that my towel chose that moment to loosen and fall. I grabbed his hand and planted it at the root of my cock. He kicked the door closed and knelt.

He looked up at me, his brown eyes framed by alabaster skin, with dark brown hair and a full pair of pink lips. He ran his hand down the length, whispering to himself in astonishment. I spoke very little Greek, but I could imagine what he said.

He lifted the tip to his mouth and kissed it. I wasn't hard yet, and my cock sagged in the middle. He used a second hand to hold it up, which turned me on. I could feel my cock grow. I was cursed with a substantial soft dick that grew to monstrous proportions. It was so big that most men turned tail and ran when they saw it come to life. It was too big for all but the most talented mouths. This guy was no match for me.

"M-may I?"

I nodded. The waiter wrapped his lips around the first inch, sucking and licking the tip. He tried to go deeper, but it was useless. His tight mouth couldn't accommodate me. As it grew longer and pushed him, he had to scoot back several inches to keep from toppling over. He nursed and slurped, running his tongue under my recently cleaned foreskin. I shivered. Even with that vast surface area, my cock was sensitive.

He looked up and smiled at me. He was proud that he had made me shake. He kept at it, and I felt two day's worth of load churning in my balls. Should I feed it to this married man? Would his wife taste it on his breath when she kissed him? Thoughts like these made me lose my erection. I pulled away, content to hold my come for a better venue. I preferred to put my gyzym in a man's ass. Oral sex was fun, but it rarely brought me to orgasm. I needed to feel my flesh engulfed in a man's backside, deep in his guts.

"Did I do it wrong?"

His question was cute.

I shook my head. "I can't come that way, that's all."

"Only with women?"

I laughed. "No, with men."

He backed away. "No. I mean, sorry, sir. That won't be possible."

I nodded. "No problem. Thank you, though."

He stood, his face red with shame. "I don't know why I did that."

I smiled. "You're not the first married man to go down there. It's normal. It's natural."

He nodded. "Yes. My uncle taught me that. But he was not so big."

I shrugged. "Nobody is this big."

He turned to leave.

I touched his shoulder. "Wait." I picked up my crumpled pants and fished in the pocket. I pulled out a fifty-drachma note. "I forgot to tip you earlier."

He pocketed the money, worth about $2.00, and smiled. "Thank you, sir." He rushed out, slamming the door behind him. I heard him say, "Sorry" from the other side of the door, and then he was gone.

I wasn't hard, but I wasn't soft, either. I pulled on my linen pants, frustrated as I had to force my cock down my right leg, only to find it straining against the fabric. I hoped it would go down enough to hide in the billowing fabric, but at that moment, it was obscene. I would be arrested for indecent exposure while fully dressed!

I thought about potato bugs. They made me squeamish, the way they looked like tiny babies with six legs. That always worked. I felt it go down. I was free to explore the ancient city.

I asked the doorman to hail me a cab for the Acropolis. A few minutes later, we were climbing the steep hill. He stopped at the entrance. Admission was a measly ten drachma, about 35 cents.

I walked the rest of the way up the hill and gazed at the Parthenon, the ancient temple to Athena, the patron Goddess of Athens. I thought for a moment of Olvera Street in Los Angeles, where a visitor can see the Avila Adobe, one of the earliest houses. It is little more than a hundred fifty years old. As I stared at that ancient structure, I yearned to live somewhere with real history. For now, it was enough to visit it as a tourist.

The other temples were in disarray. The view of the city was breathtaking, but I felt overwhelmed by the decay and ruin, reminding me of how little time I had left on Earth. I took the trail downward towards Plaka, the oldest neighborhood in Athens.

The streets in Plaka were like a maze. I zigged and zagged away from the Acropolis, passing restaurants belching delicious aromas of herbs and lamb. I was still full from breakfast, so I vowed to return at night and eat in one of the charming tavernas lining the side streets.

After two cups of tea with breakfast, I needed to pee. Across a busy street was a park with a playground full of children. I spied a restroom and made my way there. Even before I stepped inside, I knew it was a tea room. There's a smell of urine and come that wafts out of the windows.

I entered, and a dozen heads turned to make sure I wasn't a cop. The men quickly returned to fucking and sucking. I envied the men who were able to have anal sex in a restroom with no fuss. I had tried much of my life to have a quickie in public, but a dick like mine needs the privacy of a bedroom to work its magic.

I stepped to the urinal, a great big trough lined with men jacking off and watching one another. When I hauled out my schlong, they gasped. Like flies to honey, they crowded me as I struggled to piss. Hands grabbed at my cock, rude, unrelenting, hungry to worship at the altar of Priapus. A man grabbed my cock from my hand and opened his mouth, catching my piss. I was angry, and it felt good to debase him with my urine. I grabbed my manhood back, splashing the yellow wine on his face, hair, and clothes. He'd go back to his wife and try to explain his smell and mess. I shook off the last drops on his tongue, stuffed myself back into my pants, and left. As a younger man, such brazen behavior was so exciting that I could come three times at the glory hole. At this stage in my life, it bored me. I yearned for more tender kisses and slow, mind-blowing sex with a talented bottom in the privacy of my bedroom.

As I made my way back to Syntagma Square, I noticed a short young man following me. Like an American, he wore jeans and a white t-shirt, but his curly black hair and dusky skin betrayed his Greek ancestry. I slowed, closing the distance between us, then turned and smiled.

"Kalimera," I said in my best Greek.

The youth checked his watch and said, "Kalimera." I remembered it was not "hello" but "good morning." By my estimates, it was only 10:30 am. He stood facing me, his dark blue eyes adorned with long, black lashes. His chest was broad and full, made even more prominent in proportion to his short frame. As he raised his hand to shake mine, I saw muscles ripple everywhere. His bicep was as big as a Muscle Beach bodybuilder's. I enfolded his small hand in mine, marveling at how it disappeared in my grasp.

"English?"

He nodded. "A little."

"Bodybuilder?" I mimed a bicep curl with barbells.

He brightened. "Yes!"

His eyes darted downward, and he licked his lips. I looked down and saw that my beat was swollen, pressing against the fabric. The heat of the Athens sun was an aphrodisiac.

He put his hand in his back pocket and rubbed his ass. It was an unmistakable gesture. I knew a few body-builders, and they were gluttons for pain. They made excellent bottoms for my prize-winning cock because they were able to push past the agony and find ecstasy waiting on the other side.

I put a hand on my cock, just to be sure, and I saw his eyes lift slightly, indicating we had a match.

"I'm at the Grande Bretagne." I pointed to the massive hotel that loomed over Syntagma Square.

He said, "Yes. Let's go."

I felt my cock hardening and began to walk with a limp. Several passersby gasped and looked away. As we entered the hotel, the concierge rushed over. "Mr. Schutes! We have your luggage." He looked from me to the little bodybuilder at my side; then his eyes landed on my crotch. He took it all in, smiled, and winked. "We'll bring it up tonight. No need to interrupt."

I blushed, flustered by how obvious my intentions must seem to this man who has seen everything. He pursed his lips, and I realized he was an old queen. I breathed a sigh of relief, and we shared a laugh.

The rickety elevator dropped us on my floor. No sooner were we through the door when the young man tore off his shirt, revealing a body rivaling Hercules. His chest was sprinkled with a light dusting of black hair, indicating he was well on his way to adulthood. I followed suit, revealing my toned but much thinner frame.

Most encounters between men begin in anonymity. It was time to progress to the next stage of intimacy.

"I'm Peter." I wanted to be able to cry out this boy's name while I fucked him. "And you?"

"Damian." His basso profundo voice turned me on.

"Damian, let's fuck."

I was grateful my toiletries bag was in my hand luggage. I removed a tube of unscented hand cream.

He shook his head. "First, we kiss."

Oh, I was so glad to hear him say it. Nothing gets me ready like a kiss. I bent to kiss him. He grabbed my head and buried his tongue in my mouth, surprisingly intimate so early in the game. I kissed back, enjoying the rising feeling in my pants. I remembered to unbutton them before I was trapped, and they fell to my ankles. He put one hand on it, struggling to get his short fingers halfway around.

With his other hand, he undid his jeans, pulling them off by stepping on the cuffs and lifting his thick thighs out of them. I watched in fascination as the waist caught on his generous backside. As they finally came loose, I marveled at the dimples in his round, firm ass. He stroked me while we kissed. I felt his bicep brushing against my belly. He let go of my head, and his hand wandered through my furry chest hairs. He found a nipple and pinched it. I knew, from experience, that this meant he liked it, too, so I returned the favor. Oh, how that nipple rested on a mound of muscled flesh worthy of the Demi-god. His skin gave off a subtle electromagnetic aura that engulfed my hand as I rubbed and twisted his perfect tit.

Damian took my hand and planted it on his bare bottom. The energy there was twice as strong. It was a desire, a knowing, a brutal yearning for touch. I caressed his perfectly smooth bottom, allowing a finger to stray into the crack, where a few hairs tickled back.

Damian released his fingers from my nipple, then broke our kiss to suck on it. His free hand joined the one stroking my hard dick, and his fingers finally surrounded my thick flesh, touching just barely. I felt his powerful thumb running along the thick vein on my underside. My cock pulsed.

With both hands, he tugged my cock like a leash, leading me to the bed. I grabbed the tube of hand cream from the dresser and threw it onto the bed. Years of experience taught me to plan ahead.

Damian let go of me, falling back onto the bed. His penis was a tiny button, drooling precome onto his small, hairy balls. Every time I see a tiny penis, it excites me. I want to know, even for just a day, what it would be like to have nothing so heavy hanging between my legs. The smaller they are, the more I envy the man who bears no burden like mine. I understand from many conversations that they are often ashamed, but Damian was utterly unself-conscious. He knew what he liked and knew he had the ass to get it. God had designed his anatomy to be fucked by men. His penis was useless with women. It had no stalk, no means of entry. With a body like his, I knew he could have any man he wanted. And he wanted me.

He raised his powerful legs, wrapping them around my head. With his hands, he pulled apart his cheeks, then pulled my head until my mouth landed on his hole. I smelled lavender soap and testosterone. My tongue flicked playfully at the hole, wetting the black hairs surrounding it. He pulled with his legs some more, forcing my nose against the spot between his balls and ass, and my tongue had nowhere to go but up his hole. It entered easily, a good sign. He was loose.

I gathered saliva and forced it into his hole, pushing with my tongue to be sure he was good and wet. His legs relaxed, then let me go.

I stayed nose-deep in his ass, licking and spitting, stretching and sucking. His pearls of clear pre-come dribbled down his balls and onto the bridge of my nose. He was ready.

I stood, lifting my heavy cock and letting it smack into his penis. He jumped, then smiled. I did it again, and he wriggled with anticipation.

The hand cream was a recent discovery, a gift from the gods. It was thick but slippery, like a cross between cold margarine and warm Crisco. You only needed a few dabs to slick up a regular dick. I was irregular and needed a few more. But first, I put a pea-sized dollop on my finger and rubbed it on Damian's sphincter. It was not tight; my finger slipped in like a snake slithering into a leather purse.

With no resistance, I added a second, then a third finger. Damian grunted when I put in my pinky and again when my thumb joined my fist. At last, I felt resistance and knew that as loose as he was, my cock would still get the squeeze it deserved. As I pushed my arm deeper, I reached the magic door that leads to the colon, pushing in further. I wanted to know he was clean, but that lavender soap scent was all I could smell when I pulled out my hand to check. We were in business. I filled my palm with hand cream and coated my cock in long strokes.

I stepped back until my cock slipped off his body and hit my thigh before bouncing up to half-mast. It was so heavy that it rarely saw 90 degrees. When Damian pulled his cheeks wider, I could see right into his rectum. That pushed me up to 75 degrees, and I was ready. I hunched my shoulders forward to grab my cock somewhere past the halfway point and pressed the head against his throbbing hole.

As the head slid past the rectum, Damian cried out, but he didn't put a foot against my hip to stop me. Instead, he pulled his cheeks and shoved forward, taking the whole head and the first few inches of my shaft. I had found my holy grail. This ease of entry was the feeling I craved: anal sex without hours of work to get the hole open. It was easy sex, something no man over a certain size can find.

I kept pushing until I reached the junction, the spot where the rubber meets the road. If I could get my fist past there, I had a good chance of getting my cock to go there, too. Such depth was Rara Avis, a black swan. Damian's smile only got wider. There were no tears, no cries to stop. I felt that same electromagnetic pull engulfing my cock as I slipped into his colon. He tightened it with incredible muscle control. He was incredibly talented.

Damian's mouth puckered, and he leaned toward me. I saw he wanted a kiss, but I still had a few inches to go. With a deep thrust, I pushed in the last four inches, and my hips pressed against his powerful butt muscles. I leaned forward in a pushup position, hands on either side of his head, then lowered myself into his lips. Our mouths opened, and our tongues began their quest to find the deepest recesses of each other's mouths. As we kissed, I gently released my breath, and he inhaled, then exhaled into my mouth. We shared our air, renewing it with breaths through our nostrils. I was so involved in the kiss that I forgot to fuck. I was buried to the root, and I stayed there as we found ecstasy in an embrace.

Slowly, savoring every millimeter of flesh against flesh, I withdrew a few inches, then pushed forward. Damian put his legs over my shoulders to make it easier for me to maneuver. I lengthened my strokes inch by inch until my head popped through the magic door on its journey. As the strokes grew longer, I could see my head pushing his prostate, milking it, as pearly clear drops trickled from his tiny penis, wetting my pubic hair on the instroke. I dipped a finger in the nectar and put it in my mouth. The male hormones were powerful, intoxicating. I fed a helping to Damian, who obediently lapped it up.

My cock traveled from Damian's hole to the depths of his belly, pressing against his skin so we could both see the lump as it pushed forward.

Damian's guts began to churn, stroking my cock in powerful waves. His muscles were strong inside and out. His sphincter twitched, pinching my cock and releasing it in a rapid pulse. I had felt this before, but it was sometimes years before I found it again. Damian was the precious gem, a man capable of anal orgasm with something so massive inside him. I grinned as he twitched and bent, unable to stop the powerful orgasm from clenching his guts.

"Nai! Nai! Nainainainainai!" He screamed 'yes' over and over again in Greek. If the couple in the room next door were there, they got an earful. His tiny penis spewed a giant blast of semen, soaring past my head, landing in my hair. The subsequent explosion splattered my face. His ejaculations continued a half dozen more times before he ran out. The last bit just dribbled out and sat balanced on the tip of his head. I ran my finger across and fed it to him.

I was taking long, slow strokes. Damian wanted it harder, faster. I didn't know the words in Greek, but I understood him. I doubled my pace, then doubled again, until my cock was a blur. The door between realms opened and closed with a loud clapping sound. Damian threw his head from side to side, gripping the sheets and sucking air through his teeth in a whistle. He lifted a leg skyward, then twisted until he was on his side. I lay beside him, pounding his guts. The clapping grew louder, and his cries of ecstasy joined the choir in a holy hymn of ass fucking.

Every time I looked at my cock sliding past those magnificent orbs of muscle, I got closer. The tease this morning had left my balls full and angry. They yearned for release. I held one of Damian's legs aloft so I could fuck the deeply as possible. I knew that with a man this short, I could probably hit that spot where the descending colon meets the sigmoid. And I did. When that happens, it's fireworks. I hit it six or seven times until Damian began thrashing.

"Nai!" He gripped the bedspread, nearly tearing it apart with his powerful arms. I heard seams pop. His biceps bulged, and his thighs squeezed my balls. Pow! Pow! Pow! I hit that spot hard, and Damian came again. It flew off the bed, staining the carpet, then puddled on the bedspread. It was the second time he'd come without so much as touching himself. I don't remember the last time I could shoot a hands-free load. I envied his tiny, prolific penis. Still, he would never know the joys of stuffing a man's ass, let alone his colon, and at that moment, it was so fulfilling, I couldn't imagine giving it up.

Damian clenched his butt muscles, pinning my cock between them so that each stroke tugged at my cock. That was the final move, his finisher.

My balls churned. I was there. Damian rolled onto his stomach in anticipation of my impending ejaculation.

"I'm coming!"

Damian said something in Greek that must have meant, "Fill me up," because that's what happened. I held myself all the way inside. My Cowper's gland fired a massive blast that landed deep inside him. Against his tight belly flesh, I could see the glans throb as it released the first blast. It came in waves, one overtaking the other, filling him with the seeds of wisdom; old come in a young body. I collapsed on top of him, our sweat mingling.

He turned his head, and we kissed. I stayed buried deep, wondering if my hardon would ever go down.

He said, "Again."

I glanced at the wall clock. The museum would

close before I could get there. Easy sex was better than any museum.

"Okay."

We were still fucking when the concierge brought up the missing baggage. I shouted for him to leave it outside my door. I didn't care if someone came along and stole it. Damian was a flesh suitcase for my over-sized cock, all the luggage I needed.

We took a break between sessions. As we lay beside one another, smoking harsh Greek cigarettes and blowing smoke rings, the sunlight streamed through the window again, hitting the mirror and reflecting on my face as if it were early morning. It must have been a reflection from a building, but it looked like we had started the day over.

I checked my watch. It was 5:30. Sunrise? Sunset? Had we traveled through time to begin the day again? Had we fucked all night until the next morning? No, the sun was playing a trick on me. That had to be it.

Damian rolled onto his side and picked up my spent cock, rubbing the head against his cavernous hole. It slipped in soft but quickly hardened.

"Again."

It was the first time in years that I fucked someone a third time. Usually, by round two, they begged me to stop. Damian was insatiable.

I nibbled on his shoulder as I plowed into him. It was that energy coming from his skin that kept me going, exceeding my limitations, emptying my seed into him again and again. I wondered if I would ever get off this merry-go-round.

Damian was a pig for my cock. He pulled me onto my back, riding me like a cowboy sitting backward on his horse. He bent and stood like a muscleman doing squats at Gold's Gym. I watched in fascination as my towering pole disappeared and reappeared between his gluteus maximus. I caressed his tree trunk thighs, downy with wispy hair. Each squat caused his sphincter to tighten, releasing as he stood.

He said something in Greek. I only understood 'psolis' and 'megàlo,' the words for 'cock' and 'big.'

I answered, "I know."

He stood and bent over and over, faster and faster. His ass muscles grazed my pubic hair, then he straightened his legs, bringing my massive knob end right to the exit point but never letting it slip out. He spun around, twisting my cock then releasing it. He sat in my lap, bouncing in short strokes. He leaned forward, and we shared our panting breath. I held his head in my hands, my fingers hooked under his earlobes. With lips locked against mine, he bent his hips and lengthened his motion, crashing hard against my balls.

I watched my dick head travel through his belly, growing harder until, at last, I touched that magic place again. He spasmed, and contractions stroked my cock. He sat down, letting gravity force my cock deeper. His contractions gripped my cock in waves, massaging me with no effort from either party. Damian's eyes fluttered, and he shook from joy and euphoria. Beads of sweat, laden with masculine aromas, dripped from his forehead and fell to my lips. They tasted sweet and musky in equal measure, like warm waters from the rivers of delight.

We stayed together, his insides squeezing me towards orgasm. I saw his tiny penis throbbing, a loose button under pressure. I tickled it with my finger, and it spat out another load in a series of projectiles, wetting my hair, face, and chest. I marveled that such tiny balls could produce so much semen.

He roughly grabbed my nipples, twisting and squeezing them like they would give milk. He planted his mouth on my right nipple while he played with the left, his stray hand cupping my balls. I don't usually feel that powerful connection between my nipples and my cock, but the transcendent energy emanating from Damian's body sent shivers and waves of pleasure to my throbbing manhood. It was coming, a third climax, as powerful as the first and second.

"Nai," I said, "Yes. Oh, yes!"

A warm river gurgled up my shaft, filling Damian with more gyzym. By my estimates, he must have more than a teacup's worth of my seed in his belly. We waited there a few minutes until my cock softened. As I gently leaned him to the side, I shifted my hips, rapidly sliding my cock out of his hole. His ass gaped like a surprised mouth gasping for air. A warm white river flowed from his hole onto the bedspread, making a map of France. I saw the bright red flesh of his rectum, swollen and puffy.

Damian said, "Again."

By this time, I would have groaned and asked him to leave. But the energy between us was so powerful that I felt my cock rise, ready for another round. Never in my life had I done it a fourth time. Yet I knew I could with this beautiful man.

After depositing another baby in the crib, I checked the clock. Our fucking had lasted an hour, but It was still 5:30.

As I grunted fucking hard, I said, "Damian, is it morning?"

"What?"

I was perplexed; then it came to me. "Kalimera." Good morning.

"Kalimera."

A knock came at the door. "Room Service!"

I hadn't ordered breakfast. I knew if I opened the door, I would see that same married man with my full English breakfast, staring at my massive cock, now half-hard and slick with hand cream and sperm.

Time had reversed and stood still. There was no more night, only one eternal day.

ABOUT THE AUTHOR

Peter Schutes is an imaginary gay historical figure with a rich backstory. He was born in the United States in 1896. After a brief study period at Harvard University, he enlisted and fought in World War I. After the war, he was incarcerated at Napa State Mental Hospital because of his homosexuality. When he was released, he came to Hollywood, where he became a hustler.

Arrested for drug dealing, Peter escaped and fled to Kentucky. There, he worked in a coal mine, where he met his first real love. After the death of his lover, Peter retired to a bunkhouse in Montana, where he found an old typewriter and began exploring his fantasies in writing. Eventually, after laws changed, he was able to publish his gay pulp fiction books in Denmark and then the United States.

Peter returned to Los Angeles and lived out his days in the increasingly accepting society of that city. He died in Santa Monica, CA, in 1981. Except Peter Schutes didn't exist. He's a pen name.

Muscle Bottom*

Panama Heat

Satanic Seductions*

Satan's Sissy Boy

The Slaves of Rome*

The Thigh Baby

Under the Boardwalk

World's Biggest

Coming Soon

Backwoods Delivery - The Complete Daddy's Boy Series

Higher Education*

Hoboes, Hustlers, and Jailbirds*

Small Cockpits and Big Hangars*

Tales of Two Daddies*

*Available as Paperbacks

Two brazen novellas taking place in and around Ancient Greece and one short story in midcentury Athens will require a box of Kleenex by your bedside for optimal reading.

HERCULES AND LIPPOS features the hunky demigod and his overly blessed companion, Lippos. Together, the two men go on adventures, both geographical and sexual. Antiquity never felt so hot.

THE GOSPEL OF PRIAPUS is a pseudo-mythical religious text that recounts the life of Priapus, the great phallic god, and his tiny companion Chrysion. The text includes instructions for establishing a temple of phallic worship in your city.

ONE ETERNAL DAY is a modern story set in Athens. The immense protagonist, Peter, meets an extraordinarily muscular youth with a small problem, and together they turn the clocks back.